1754

. . . Rebecca shivered slightly
and looked for signs of movement
in the fort. Her mouth went dry with fear.
She took a deep breath and began to explore
the fort's dark Yard. Cautiously, she hurried from one
doorway to the next. She could not risk the guards
seeing her and questioning why she was outside
in the middle of the night. She was just a short
distance from Widow Tyler's cabin
when she saw a shadowy figure
walking toward her. . . .

REBECCA'S WORLD
New Hampshire in 1754

Fort Number 4

Great Chamber

South Gate

Connecticut River

ENEMY
IN THE FORT

❦

by
Sarah Masters Buckey

American Girl™

Printed in the United States of America.
01 02 03 04 05 06 RRD 10 9 8 7 6 5 4 3 2 1

History Mysteries® and American Girl®
are trademarks of Pleasant Company.

PERMISSIONS & PICTURE CREDITS
The following individuals and organizations have generously given permission to reprint
illustrations contained in "A Peek into the Past": p. 157—©Lee Snider/CORBIS; pp. 158-159—
attack, North Wind Picture Archives; Fort No. 4, ©Lee Snider/CORBIS; painting of village,
neg. #312686 (photo by H.S. Rice), courtesy Dept. of Library Services, American Museum
of Natural History; pp. 160-161—wampum and shells provided by www.wampumworks.com;
march of prisoners, courtesy of The Edward E. Ayer Collection, Newberry Library, Chicago;
Susanna Johnson, Billings Family Archives, Billings Farm and Museum, Woodstock, VT; Indian
man holding child, North Wind Picture Archives; pp. 162-163—Cornplanter, State Historical
Society of Wisconsin, Rare Book Collection; statue of Mary Jemison, photo by Charlotte
Letkemann; glassblower, The Corning Museum of Glass, Corning, NY; Fort Laramie (detail) by
Alfred J. Miller, 1851, The Thomas Gilcrease Institute of American History and Art, Tulsa.

Cover and Map Illustrations: Douglas Fryer
Line Art: Greg Dearth

Library of Congress Cataloging-in-Publication Data

Buckey, Sarah Masters, 1955-.
Enemy in the Fort / by Sarah Masters Buckey. — 1st ed.
p. cm. — (History mysteries ; 13)
"American girl."
Summary: In 1754, with her own parents taken captive, twelve-year-old Rebecca must
confront her fear and hatred of the Abenaki when a boy raised by members of that tribe
is brought to the fort at Charlestown, New Hampshire, just before a series of thefts occurs.

ISBN 1-58485-307-7 — ISBN 1-58485-306-9 (pbk.)
[1. Frontier and pioneer life—New Hampshire—Fiction. 2. Indian captivities—Fiction.
3. Abenaki Indians—Fiction. 4. Indians of North America—Canada, Eastern—Fiction.
5. New Hampshire—History—Colonial period, ca. 1600-1775—Fiction.
6. Mystery and detective stories.] I. Title. II. Series.

PZ7.B87983 En 2001   [Fic]—dc21   00-046518

To Jay

TABLE OF CONTENTS

ATTACKED

Spring 1752

Rebecca Percy peered into the darkness, listening, wondering. Moments before, she had been lost in deep sleep. Now her eyes were wide open. What had awakened her?

It wasn't her younger sister, Selinda. She lay asleep, tightly curled beside Rebecca in the narrow bed they shared.

It wasn't the dawn. Looking out the attic window near their bed, Rebecca could see that the moon had set, but the sun had not yet begun to rise. Stars were sprinkled across the spring sky. They blinked like cats' eyes peering out from the darkness, far, far away.

Perhaps 'twas the wind that woke me, Rebecca thought.

A chilling wind was blowing down from Canada through the forests of northern New England. Rebecca could hear leaves shuffle and branches creak in the wind. Somewhere in the woods, a wolf howled mournfully.

Nothing seemed out of the ordinary.

A gust of wind chilled the attic loft and gave Rebecca goose bumps. She lay back in bed and tugged on the quilt, but it wouldn't budge. Selinda had wound herself in the bedcover like a spindle wrapped in thread. Carefully, Rebecca unwound her sister and arranged the quilt so that it covered them both.

She was about to nestle her head in her feather pillow when she heard a snarl from downstairs. It was Virgil, the Percys' big black-and-white watchdog. He was pacing the length of the cabin's main room, and he was growling a deep, threatening growl.

Rebecca started up in bed again. *Could something— or someone—be outside?*

Her parents must have awakened, too, for now Rebecca could hear them whispering to each other and moving about downstairs. She heard her father, Josiah Percy, lift his musket from the two pegs where it hung above the front door.

Rebecca crept out of bed and over to the edge of the sleeping loft, where she could peer down at her parents. Embers from the evening's fire still glowed in the fireplace. Rebecca could see that her father had pulled on his breeches and was looking out a crack between the window shutters. Virgil was pacing in front of the cabin door, like a soldier on sentry duty. His sharp claws scratched against the wide wooden planks of the floor.

"Mama," Rebecca called down softly. She was careful not to wake Selinda or their baby brother, Benjamin, who slept in a cradle near their parents' bed. "What is it?"

Mama looked up toward the loft. She was a small, energetic woman with dark eyes and brown curls that reached past her waist. She had thrown a shawl over her night shift. "Hush, child," she whispered. Then she turned to her husband. "Should we hasten to the fort, Josiah?" she asked in a low tone.

It must be Indians! Rebecca thought.

Fort Number 4, about a quarter-mile away, had been built to protect the English colonists from the Indians. Whenever there was a threat of attack, the Percys and other families could take shelter inside the fort. Now Rebecca watched her father anxiously, waiting for his decision.

She saw him shake his head, then put a finger to his lips. With a shock, Rebecca realized it might be too late for the family to escape to the fort. Indians could be somewhere close by, maybe even in the farmyard.

Suddenly, Virgil's growl turned to furious barking. He charged at the front door as if he would rip it from its hinges. Awakened by the dog, baby Benjamin started to cry, a loud, insistent bawling.

"Rebecca, fetch your sister," Mama whispered. "And you both come down. Now."

Rebecca hurried to the bed that she shared with

Selinda. "Wake up! Mama says to come downstairs."

"What?" Selinda mumbled. "Is it morning?"

"No, but . . ." Rebecca paused. She didn't want to frighten her sister, but she *had* to hurry. "It might be Indians."

"Rebecca! Selinda!" Mama's voice was quiet but urgent. "Come quick!"

Rebecca scrambled down the ladder to the main room, and Selinda, who walked with a limp, followed close behind. Their mother was standing by the trapdoor that led to the Percys' root cellar. Usually, a blue rag rug covered the door, but Mama had pushed the rug aside. Now she pulled open the door.

"Hide in there," she told the girls. "Hurry!"

Rebecca protested. "But, Mama . . ."

Papa glanced away from the window. He was a big, broad-shouldered man who often laughed with his daughters and told them merry stories. But tonight he looked deadly serious. "Mind your mother!" he ordered in a low voice. "And don't say a word, no matter what you hear. Understand?"

Rebecca nodded. "Yes, sir," she whispered.

Selinda, still dazed from sleep, looked bewildered. "Mama, what about you?" she asked. "And Ben?"

"The savages would hear Ben's crying," Mama whispered. "I must stay with your father. You girls hide together. And remember, be quiet!"

Both girls knew that when Mama made up her mind, there was no point arguing. Selinda climbed down the cellar ladder, then crouched down on the cellar floor, her skinny arms wrapped around her knees. Rebecca followed her sister. Her bare feet had just touched the cellar's chilly floor when Mama called to her softly. "Becca!"

She looked up. Mama was leaning over the trapdoor entrance. In her hands she held the family's most prized possession: a pair of silver spoons.

The beautiful engraved spoons had belonged to Mama's mother. They had been brought all the way from England when Mama was a little girl. Ever since Rebecca could remember, the two spoons had been kept in a special box underneath Mama and Papa's bed. They were taken out only on very special occasions. Now Mama reached down low and handed the precious spoons to Rebecca.

"Here," she said, her dark eyes looking straight into Rebecca's. "Keep these. And watch over your sister. I'm counting on you." Mama bit her lip, as if she wanted to say more but could not trust herself. Abruptly, she stood up and closed the trapdoor.

The two sisters heard a heavy *whoosh* as their mother dragged the rag rug over the entrance. They huddled together in the small, pitch-black cellar. It was cold and damp, and it smelled of parsnips and potatoes. Rebecca felt her sister begin to tremble. She put her arm around Selinda's bony shoulders and pulled her close.

They could hear the dog barking and baby Benjamin's insistent crying, but for several minutes, that was all they could hear. Then there was a loud pounding on the door, followed by the crash of the cabin door bursting open.

Virgil's barking grew even more ferocious. There was a scuffle somewhere above their heads and a terrible thud. Then Virgil was silent.

"What . . ." Selinda whispered.

Rebecca clamped her hand over her sister's mouth. "Shhhhhh!"

Terrified, the girls listened to the tromping of feet above them. They heard Indians shouting commands. Then they heard Papa's voice. Josiah Percy sometimes traded with his Abenaki Indian neighbors, and he spoke a little of their language. Now he sounded calm, as if he were trying to make a deal with the men who had invaded his home.

But the Indians seemed angry. Rebecca could hear banging and crashing above her head. Baby Benjamin continued his wild wailing. Mrs. Percy spoke to her son in a loud, clear voice that rose above the din. "Don't cry, angel. We must go with these men, but we'll be all right. The Lord will watch over us, and someday we'll come back here. You must be quiet now."

Why does Mama speak in such a way to Benjamin? Rebecca wondered in confusion. *He's only a baby. He can't understand!*

Then Rebecca understood. Mama wasn't really talking to Benjamin at all. She meant her words to be overheard by her daughters. The Indians were taking Mama, Papa, and Benjamin away, and she and Selinda were to stay hidden until they were gone!

Rebecca clenched Selinda tightly. She felt her sister's body heave with silent sobbing. Footsteps hurried above them, sometimes right over their heads. One moment, Rebecca was terrified that their hiding place would be discovered and the Indians would capture them. Then she was terrified that she and Selinda would be left alone. Without Mama and Papa, what would they do?

In the cabin above them, a man issued what sounded like a command. Then, almost as quickly as they had arrived, the Indians left, taking Mama, Papa, and Benjamin as their prisoners.

Suddenly, the cabin was quiet.

For Rebecca, the silence was even more horrible than the raid. She recalled the many tales she'd heard of Indian attacks. After the Indians took their prisoners, they often returned to set fire to their captives' farms.

She leaned over to whisper in her sister's ear, "Selinda, we must get away from here!"

As Rebecca moved, the spoons jangled in her lap. "Hold these," she said. She handed the spoons to Selinda. Then she climbed up to the trapdoor and put her ear to it. There was no sound above. Holding on to the ladder with one hand, she pushed with her free hand, but the door did not yield. *What if we can't get out?* she thought in panic. *Will this be our grave?*

Bracing her feet against the ladder, Rebecca used both hands to push as hard as she could. The heavy wooden door swung open, with the rug dangling above it.

"Come quickly!" she whispered to Selinda. Together, the girls emerged from the cellar.

Selinda gasped. Their home had been ransacked. Mama and Papa's bed had been torn apart, and the table was up-ended. All of Mama's tidy housekeeping was destroyed.

Rebecca grabbed her sister's arm. "Hurry! We'll hide in Fairyland."

She pulled Selinda out the broken door and dragged her across the yard to the small cluster of pine trees they had long ago named Fairyland. Between the trees, the ground dipped in a deep hollow. It was a sheltered spot only a few dozen yards from the cabin, and it had always been one of their favorite places to play.

When they reached the pine-scented hollow, they peered out into the shadows of the surrounding woods. "Look!" whispered Selinda. She pointed toward the edge of the farmyard. Two Indian men carrying torches were coming toward the cabin.

"Be quiet!" Rebecca hissed. "Don't say a word or they'll find us."

The Indians set fire to the Percys' home and barn,

then retreated back into the northern woods. Horrified, the two girls watched as flames shot up from their farmstead. Waves of heat spread from the blaze, and the girls almost choked from the thick smoke.

Then, over the cracking of burning timbers, Rebecca heard the boom of the great gun from Fort Number 4. "They've sighted the smoke," she whispered to Selinda. "The soldiers will be here soon."

By the time the soldiers from the fort arrived, dawn was streaking the sky. The Percys' house was a mass of smoking ashes. Only parts of the cabin's floor and a few charred logs of the foundation remained.

It was Captain Phineas Stevens, the commander of Fort Number 4, who found the girls in their hiding place. "Come out," he told them. His face looked stern, but his voice was kind. "The Indians are gone."

Rebecca wanted to cry, but the tears would not come. She felt as if someone had put a cork in her heart, and her feelings were stuck inside. She stood up and held out her hand for her sister. "Come, Selinda, we must go."

Selinda did not answer. She sat motionless in the hollow, one hand clutching the silver spoons. Her eyes looked as blank as two brown buttons.

"Please, Selinda!" Rebecca pleaded.

Still, Selinda did not move.

Without a word, Captain Stevens stepped down into the hollow. Gently, he picked Selinda up and carried her to his horse. She drooped on the saddle like a rag doll.

"I'll take you to the fort," the captain told Rebecca as he helped her onto the horse behind her sister. "You'll be safe there, and I wager you'll be able to stay with Widow Tyler for a while—least till we can find you another home."

"What about Mama and Papa and Ben?" Rebecca protested. "The savages took them captive. We must help them!"

Captain Stevens shook his head. "All we can do now is wait and pray that the Abenakis'll trade your family back to us someday—either for money or for Indians we've taken prisoner." He shook his head sadly. "Just wait and pray." He tugged on his horse's reins, and they started off through the dark forest toward the fort.

As they rode away, Rebecca turned to look at the smoldering ruins that had once been her home. *I'll never forgive those savages,* she vowed. *Not as long as I live.*

CHAPTER I

A CAPTIVE RETURNS

August 1754

Rebecca stood tiptoe on a bench inside Widow Tyler's cabin. More than two years had passed since the raid on her family's farm. She was now twelve years old and, as Widow Tyler was fond of saying, "almost as tall as a woman grown."

It was warm in the widow's cabin, and the room smelled like apple cider. A damp strand of hair dangled in Rebecca's face, but she couldn't brush it aside. Her hands were full of long strings of apple rings. She had peeled and cored a bushel of apples and sliced the apples into rings. Then she had set the rings out in the sun, and after they were partly dried, she had strung them onto heavy thread. Now the rings were ready for hanging.

By standing on the bench, Rebecca could reach the broad rafters that supported the ceiling. She stretched as tall as she could and looped the strings of apple rings along rafters near the cabin's wide fireplace. She carefully positioned the strings so that the fire's heat would slowly dry the apples into leathery circles. When she was finished, puckered apple rings bobbed overhead like beads strung on a lady's necklace.

Rebecca looked up at her work, and she remembered the rhyme her mother had taught her years before:

> *If you dry your apples in the fall,*
> *When winter comes, there'll be pie for all.*

I wonder where Mama is now, she thought with a stab of sorrow. *Or Papa or baby Benjamin? Are they alive or . . .*

Rebecca bit her lip. *There's no time for such thoughts,* she reminded herself. *I must get things ready so we don't go hungry this winter.* She stirred the bean soup that was simmering on the fire and wondered what to do next. Should she braid the onions and hang them in the loft where she and Selinda slept? Should she pickle the cucumbers?

She glanced over at Widow Tyler, who was sleeping in her chair. She wished the widow would wake up and advise her about what chores should be done first. But the widow had been ill and she slept deeply. A quilt had fallen from her lap, and it lay bunched on the cabin's floor.

Rebecca leaned down and picked up the quilt. She noticed it was stained. "I'll wash it soon," she promised herself. She folded it neatly, then put it on top of the wooden trunk where the widow kept her clothes and blankets.

As Rebecca stood up, she glanced out the front window. It opened into the middle of Fort Number 4, a small, guarded village of about one hundred and eighty colonists. The families of the fort had built their wooden cabins and lean-tos around a central public square, called the Yard. The homes were built side by side so that there were no gaps between them and each building offered protection to its neighbors.

A grassy area lay behind the cabins on the east, west, and north sides of the fort. The settlers used this area for woodpiles, outhouses, small gardens, and laundry set out to dry. Just beyond the grassy area, a tall palisade stood as a fence between the fort and the wilderness. The palisade was made of logs, each over fourteen feet high, that stood upright in the ground about four to five inches apart. They were close enough together so that attackers could not pass between them, but far enough apart so that if attackers set one log on fire, the flames would not spread easily to the next log.

On the south side of the fort, the Great Chamber stood above the South Gate. In times of peace, the settlers held church services and town councils in the Great Chamber. In times of war, the chamber was a barracks for soldiers, and muskets boomed from its narrow windows. A tall watchtower rose up from one side of the Great Chamber.

It overlooked the fort and the surrounding countryside. Beneath the watchtower, soldiers guarded the South Gate, the fort's only entrance.

Ever since the raid, Rebecca and Selinda had lived inside the fort with Widow Tyler, who had kindly offered to share her home with the sisters. The widow was a poor woman who did sewing for other settlers. Under the widow's teaching, Selinda had become a very good seamstress. Because she was lame—the result of a broken leg that had never healed quite right—Selinda did not mind sitting quietly for hours at a time. She would work patiently on a dress until it was perfect.

Rebecca had little of her sister's patience, but she was strong and willing to work hard. She cleaned, cooked, and did chores for the widow and other families who needed occasional help. By working together, she, Selinda, and the widow had earned enough money to survive during their first year together.

Last spring, however, the widow had become ill, and she'd had to give up her sewing. Since then, Rebecca had spent most of her time nursing the widow and taking care of the house. Eleven-year-old Selinda had been hired out to work for the Cutters, a family from Connecticut who had recently moved to the fort. In the evenings, Selinda helped Rebecca with chores at home.

At least Selinda and I still have each other, Rebecca thought as she looked out the window to the warm sunshine outside. On this bright August day, the fort's Yard was filled with activity. Women in work dresses hurried about their errands, men armed with muskets talked and traded, and a gang of little children screeched and shouted in a noisy game of blindman's bluff.

Rebecca wished with all her heart that she could be outside, too. But she knew she had chores to do. *I'd best be starting on the pickles,* she decided. With a grimace, she remembered how much she hated the sour smell of the pickling vinegar.

She sighed and was about to turn back to her work when she caught sight of her sister. Selinda was crossing the Yard with her arms full of quilts. Fifteen-year-old Ezekiel Cutter walked ahead of Selinda. They were making their way toward the South Gate. Rebecca realized they must be headed down to the river to do washing.

I could go with them and wash the widow's quilt, Rebecca thought. *It would be so pleasant to step into the cool river . . .*

She glanced at Widow Tyler. The old woman was still asleep. *I'll do the pickles later,* Rebecca decided. She grabbed the stained quilt and hurried outside. "Selinda, tarry a moment! I'll go with you!"

Rebecca ran across the Yard, the baked ground feeling hot under her bare feet. When she reached her sister, she was surprised to see that Selinda looked pale and that her eyes were red from crying.

"What troubles you?" Rebecca asked breathlessly.

Selinda looked up sadly. Both girls were slender, with walnut-brown eyes and curly, dark brown hair. But while Rebecca had grown tall, Selinda was frail and small for her age. "Oh, Becca . . ." Selinda began.

She stopped as Ezekiel turned and walked toward them. He was a tall, broad-shouldered boy with red hair and a jaw that jutted out like a bulldog's. Although he was too young to be a soldier, he liked to think of himself as a tough Indian fighter. He wore his long hunting knife in a leather sheath, and he carried his musket proudly.

"I'll tell you later, when we're alone," Selinda whispered.

"Can't you hurry?" Ezekiel demanded, staring at Selinda. "I have better things to do than stand watch over a servant girl."

"I'm going with you to the river," Rebecca announced. Ezekiel was about to protest, so she continued. "I can help Selinda, and we'll be safer if we all go together."

"Oh, very well," Ezekiel agreed reluctantly. "But don't keep me waiting." He walked ahead, leaving the girls to follow.

"Yes, Your Majesty!" Rebecca muttered behind his back. She turned to her sister. "Here, I'll carry one of those," she said, and took one of the two quilts from Selinda's arms.

They crossed the Yard and passed under the South Gate. "Be careful out there," cautioned the sentry, a young private named Jacob Chandler. "You know what folks've been saying."

Rebecca felt herself tighten with anxiety. Since the attack on the Percys' farm, Fort Number 4 had enjoyed a relatively peaceful period. Yet recently there had been growing rumors that the French and Indians were once again preparing to attack.

Fort Number 4's location made it a target for Indian raids. The small fort was isolated on the edge of the New England colonies. To the north of the fort lay vast miles of forests, rivers, and mountains controlled by the Indians and their French allies in Canada. To the south, the next closest English fort was fifty miles away. There was no road between the forts. English colonists traveled between the two outposts either by canoe or by forest trails. Either way, it was a dangerous journey.

"If I see a savage, I'll shoot him dead," Ezekiel bragged.

"Well," said Private Chandler, "I wouldn't want to be the one to tell Miss Priscilla that something had happened to you." Priscilla was Ezekiel's blue-eyed older sister. She was thought by many people—including Private Chandler— to be the prettiest girl in the fort.

"Keep your eyes open," the private warned.

Ezekiel led the way through the gate, with Rebecca and Selinda following close behind. They left the safety of the high palisade behind and started down the trail to the Connecticut River, less than half a mile away.

The well-worn path led across the wide meadows and then through the woods. Rebecca breathed deeply as she walked through the meadows. She loved the smell of flowers, and all around her were graceful goldenrod, cheerful black-eyed Susans, and delicate Queen Anne's lace. Honeybees darted among the blossoms.

Rebecca spied some blackberry bushes near the trail. Their thorny branches were dotted with ripe, luscious-looking fruit. Rebecca stopped for a moment and shifted the quilts to her left arm. She quickly picked as many of the berries as she could hold in her right hand. She ate a few of the juicy, slightly tart berries, then offered some to Selinda. The younger girl shook her head.

"Oh, I forgot," Rebecca said, recalling that berries gave her sister a rash. "I'm sorry." She was about to eat the remaining berries herself when Ezekiel grabbed them from her hand.

"I'll take those," he said, and stuffed the berries in his mouth. Juice dribbled down his chin.

"Those were mine!" Rebecca protested.

Ezekiel smiled meanly. "Now they're mine," he said. He scanned the late-afternoon sky. "Hurry up! We've only a few more hours of light left, and you girls've been going slower than molasses in January."

Rebecca looked up at him defiantly. "We'd go quicker if you'd carry one of these," she said, holding out the two big quilts in her arms. "And besides . . ."

"Wait!" Selinda grabbed her sister's hand. "Someone's coming!"

Rebecca and Ezekiel whirled around. Rebecca caught her breath. A man on horseback was galloping toward them. Ezekiel reached for his musket.

"Don't shoot!" a hoarse voice shouted. "It's me, Old Johnny."

Rebecca breathed easily again. All the fort's residents knew Old Johnny. He was a peddler who traveled to settlements throughout the New England colonies. Every few months, he visited Fort Number 4 to trade, drink rum, and share the latest news.

Ezekiel lowered his musket. "Didn't know it was you, Johnny. We don't get many visitors."

Johnny pulled his horse up in front of them. He was a small, thin man with an overgrown beard. "You'll get more visitors soon," he rasped. "I met up with Cap'n Stevens and his men a few hours ago."

Captain Stevens! Rebecca and Selinda exchanged excited glances. Both girls had the same thought: *Maybe he has news for us!*

The governor of the Massachusetts Bay Colony had sent Captain Stevens to Canada to ransom English captives being held in Montréal. The captain had been chosen for the mission because he himself was a former Indian captive. The Abenakis had captured him when he was in his teens, and he had learned their language and customs. After he was ransomed, the captain had returned to the English colonies. He had become a leader who was respected for his courage and his knowledge of the Indians.

Now everyone in the fort was eager for the captain's return from his latest mission—especially the Percy sisters.

"When's the captain gettin' here, Johnny?" Ezekiel asked.

The peddler shrugged. "He said he'd be home by sunset today, but first he was going to parley with some Indians he'd heard was nearby." The peddler wiped his chin with a dirty sleeve. "I figured I'd come ahead to the fort and have a drink or two."

"Does Captain Stevens have anyone with him—any captives?" Rebecca asked eagerly.

Johnny nodded. "Aye, he does."

Selinda squeezed her sister's hand. "Is it a man and a woman—with a little boy?" she asked, her eyes bright with hope.

"Nay," said Johnny. "Just a boy, and he's about fourteen or so. He's been with the Abenakis most of his life. And from what I heard tell, he weren't too keen on leaving them, either."

"He might've seen Mama or Papa in an Indian village," Selinda said hopefully. "He might know where they are."

The peddler shrugged. "The cap'n ought to reach the

fort soon. Then you can ask the boy yourself—if he'll tell you. Farewell!" He snapped his horse's reins and rode off.

Ezekiel motioned to the girls to hurry. "'Tisn't safe out here! Make haste."

With Ezekiel in the lead, they proceeded single file down the trail. The path led through the woods, then dipped down a steep embankment to the river. Rebecca was filled with excitement. She could hardly wait to talk with Captain Stevens!

When they reached the water's edge, Ezekiel pointed toward a tree. "I'll be there. Holler if you see anything. And work quick!"

Rebecca tucked up the hem of her homespun petticoat and waded out into the river. The chilly water lapped against her bare legs. She splashed a little on her flushed face and felt a cooling trickle down her back.

"Get to work!" Ezekiel shouted from his shady perch.

Rebecca glared at him. Then she rolled up her sleeves and started pounding the quilts against stones along the riverbank. "Ezekiel angers me so!" she told Selinda in a low tone. "But 'tis exciting about the captain's return, is it not?"

For a moment, Selinda said nothing. Rebecca glanced up from the quilts and saw tears welling in her sister's eyes. "What ails you? Tell me!"

"'Tis the Cutters," Selinda said at last. "They've decided to move back to Connecticut. Mrs. Cutter says it's too dangerous here. They plan to leave a week from Friday."

Rebecca was relieved. "Ah, is that it? Well, I never gave a fig for the Cutters anyhow. Ezekiel is a bully, and his sister Priscilla is vainer than a peacock. She keeps you sewing all day just so she can swish around the fort looking pretty." Rebecca gave the Cutters' quilt an extra-hard pounding. "Don't fret, we'll find you work somewhere else."

"You don't understand," protested Selinda. "*I* must go, too."

"What!" Rebecca was so startled that she dropped the quilt. It splashed into the water. "What do you mean?"

"Mrs. Cutter says I'm indentured to her, so I must leave with them."

"But we had an agreement!" Rebecca exclaimed. "When you were hired out to them, Mrs. Cutter said you'd only work for them during the day, and you and I could still live together at the widow's. She promised!"

"Now Mrs. Cutter says everything's changed 'cause they're moving. She says she paid for a year of my service and by law I'm bound to give it." Selinda looked up at her sister. "Oh, Becca! Connecticut's so far! If they take me there, I might never see you again!" She paused and her face crumpled into tears. "And what if Mama and Papa come back—and I'm gone?"

Rebecca felt shaken. Neither she nor Selinda could remember ever traveling more than a few miles from Fort Number 4—much less all the way to Connecticut. How could Mrs. Cutter take Selinda away? The two sisters had never spent even a night apart. Would Mrs. Cutter really separate them—maybe forever?

Suddenly, all the beauty of the late-summer day vanished for Rebecca. Despite the hot sun, she felt cold all over. But she saw Selinda looking up at her with worried eyes. Rebecca tried to smile. "We'll think of something," she promised as she pounded the wet wool on the rocks. "We'll ask Captain Stevens for help. Don't worry."

By the time they arrived back at the fort, the sun had begun to dip behind the trees. The sentry told them that Captain Stevens had been sighted off in the distance—about half an hour's ride away. Rebecca and Selinda quickly set the quilts out to dry in the grassy area behind the cabins. Then they hurried to join the excited crowd of settlers who were gathering in the Yard. Soon the loud cracks of muskets split the air.

"Huzzah! Welcome back!" the settlers shouted as the captain and his soldiers rode in through the South Gate. A lean, darkly tanned boy followed close behind the soldiers. Rebecca knew he must be the former captive. She watched him eagerly.

He rode his big horse with careless grace, his bare feet dangling outside the stirrups. He had greasy brown hair that hung down past his shoulders, and his face was smudged with dirt. His clothes—an oversized homespun shirt and baggy breeches—looked as if they were castoffs from the soldiers.

The soldiers waved and shouted greetings to their friends and family. The boy ignored the hubbub around him. He stared straight ahead, expressionless.

Rebecca's heart fell as she watched the boy. *He doesn't look like a real white boy at all,* she thought. *He looks like an Indian in a white man's skin.*

Behind her, she heard Ezekiel spit on the hard-packed earth. "That one's trouble," he muttered darkly. "Mark my words."

CHAPTER 2
THE WHITE INDIAN

Captain Stevens' beard had grown more gray since Rebecca had last seen him, but otherwise he looked the same. He was a muscular man of middle height with a barrel chest and a ready smile. He warmly greeted his friends and family. Then he motioned to the boy.

"This lad's name is Isaac Davidson," the captain announced. "He was captured by the Abenakis 'bout eight years ago. The Indians killed most all of his family, but they adopted Isaac into their tribe."

The captain paused, and Rebecca shifted nervously from one foot to the other. Ever since the raid on her family's farm, her greatest hope had been that the Indians would someday sell Mama, Papa, and Benjamin to the French. The French might then ransom them back to the English—either for money or in exchange for French or Indian prisoners.

But not all captives were ransomed. Although Rebecca tried hard not to think about it, she knew that some captives were killed by the Indians and some died on the long, hard march to Canada. Other captives, like Isaac, were adopted by the Indians and raised as members of their tribe.

Looking at Isaac, Rebecca couldn't help thinking about her baby brother. *Mayhap Benjamin is growing up with an Indian family right now,* she thought. *Mayhap . . .*

Captain Stevens' booming voice broke in on her thoughts. "A few months ago, Isaac's tribe met up with some of our soldiers," the captain continued. "There was a battle, and afterward the soldiers found young Isaac among the Indians taken prisoner. The soldiers discovered that the boy still has kin—an aunt and uncle living in New York. His kinfolk want him back, so we're keeping Isaac here till they travel up and claim him."

A murmur spread through the crowd. Several people pressed toward Isaac. They had friends or family who had been captured by the Indians, and they hoped for news of their loved ones. One woman tugged at the sleeve of the boy's homespun shirt. "Have you heard of a girl called Hope Adams?" she implored. "She was taken four summers ago, just south of here."

Isaac's face showed no emotion. He shook his arm free from the woman's grasp, but she continued her plea. "She's my niece, and she'd be ten years old now. She had bright red curls. Have you seen a girl like that?"

Selinda whispered to her sister, "Perchance he's seen Mama or Papa or baby Benjamin! Let's ask him."

"Wait," Rebecca whispered back. She watched Isaac as he ignored the woman. His horse, spooked by the crowd, reared up. Isaac did nothing to control it, and the crowd backed away.

A soldier grabbed the horse's reins and steadied it. Several people in the crowd began talking among themselves. "That boy's been too long with the Indians," Rebecca heard one man say to his friend. "Looks to me like he's become a savage himself."

"Aye," his friend agreed. "I don't know about having him here in the fort—it's like invitin' a fox into the henhouse."

Rebecca stiffened. *Could this savage boy be a danger to the fort?*

Captain Stevens' voice rose above the crowd. "Everyone should understand it's been a long time since Isaac's been with his own people. He speaks Indian now and a little French. He's forgotten all the English he ever knew. And he's grown up thinking that we're the enemy. It's up to us to show him different."

The captain smiled wearily at the crowd of settlers. "We need someone to give the boy a home till his kin come to claim him. It'll only be for a few weeks. Any volunteers?"

Mrs. Randolph, the shopkeeper's wife, stood in front of Rebecca. She told her husband, "I wouldn't sleep easy with a boy like that in our house. I'd be afraid he'd attack us in the night." Mr. Randolph nodded in agreement.

I feel sorry for whoever takes that boy in, Rebecca thought. She glanced around to see who the unlucky family might be. No one stepped forward.

"It would be an act of Christian charity," Captain Stevens urged.

Suddenly, a woman's voice piped up from the back of the crowd. "The boy can stay with me!"

Startled, Rebecca turned around. It was Widow Tyler who had spoken! *She must have awakened from her nap feeling better,* Rebecca realized. *But why would she invite this savage boy into our home?*

The widow walked forward. She was a thin woman, and she had once been tall, but now her back was stooped with age. Ever since her illness, she had suffered bad times when she was tired and forgetful. But she also had good times, when she seemed almost as vigorous as she'd once been. This was one of her good times. There was a touch of color in her pale cheeks, and her voice was firm. The crowd separated for her as she drew up to Captain Stevens.

She smiled at him. "We have missed you, Phineas. Welcome back." The widow was hard of hearing, and she spoke with a piercing voice. As a longtime resident

of the fort, she was one of the few people who called
Captain Stevens by his first name.

He bowed slightly to the widow. "'Tis good to be back,
Abigail, and I'm glad to see you've recovered from your
ailments." He gestured at Isaac. "Are you sure you're ready
to take on this young man?"

Widow Tyler nodded. "It's worked out well enough
having the Percy girls." She paused briefly and coughed,
then gathered her strength again. "And what is one
mouth more?"

"Thank ye, Abigail," Captain Stevens said with a smile,
and the issue of Isaac's lodging was decided. Rebecca felt
filled with dread, but the other settlers relaxed. They began
peppering Captain Stevens with questions.

"What news have ye?" one farmer called out. "Are the
Indians up to trouble again?"

Captain Stevens looked grave. He told the crowd that
there had been an attack near the Merrimack River. The
Malloon family had been captured.

Another family destroyed by those savages, Rebecca thought
angrily.

"We've enjoyed peace for a good while, but it looks
as if it's coming to an end," Captain Stevens warned the
crowd. "Everyone who's living on farms outside the fort
should consider moving in. And no one should travel
beyond the fort unless absolutely necessary."

Old Johnny yelled out from the crowd. "What if our

business *is* travel?" he asked. "What good is a peddler who
stays in one place?"

"Then you're responsible for your own safety; the
soldiers of this fort will not guard you," Captain Stevens
told him sternly.

"As if they ever did," Johnny mumbled.

"And for everyone's safety, no one should leave the fort
without a guard," Captain Stevens continued. "Especially
at night."

"I believe in being safe as much as the next man, but
there's no call to live like we're in prison," called out James
Johnson, a farmer with a soft Irish accent. "My family is
staying on our farm. As a matter of fact, Mrs. Johnson and
I are having a wee party Friday night."

Several people cheered. Mr. Johnson smiled. "Bring
your muskets, but prepare to have a good time!"

Captain Stevens frowned. "This is no laughing matter.
Everyone must be watchful. Now excuse me. I'll settle
Isaac at the Widow Tyler's."

The crowd broke up. Selinda had to return to the
Cutters with Ezekiel. Rebecca followed Captain Stevens,
Widow Tyler, and the savage boy back to the widow's cabin.

The log house was made up of one main room with a
small sleeping loft above it. The big fireplace stood across
from the cabin's front door. A long oak table, flanked by
benches on either side, sat near the hearth. To the left
of the door was the widow's bed, which was partitioned

off from the rest of the room by curtains.

Widow Tyler pointed at her bed. "We'll take the trundle bed from under my bed and put it over there," she said, motioning to the far corner of the room.

Rebecca was surprised to see the widow's new energy. *It's almost as if she's glad the savage boy will be staying here,* Rebecca thought.

They carried the low trundle bed from underneath the widow's tall bed to the empty corner of the room. The widow opened her trunk and pulled out a pair of thin, patched blankets. She showed Rebecca how to hang the old blankets from the rafters so that they enclosed the two open sides of the bed. The blankets did not reach all the way to the floor, but they offered a measure of privacy.

Isaac sat cross-legged on the floor as they worked. When they were finished, Captain Stevens spoke in Abenaki to the boy. Isaac muttered a reply.

"I told him this is where he'll sleep, and that he's to help you with chores," Captain Stevens explained.

The widow nodded. "That'd be fine," she said. "We need some wood chopped."

Again Captain Stevens spoke to the boy. Isaac fired back what sounded like a question. "He wants to know if there's food," Captain Stevens translated.

The widow smiled. "I know what hungry boys are like. Why, my son Ethan could eat enough for four men when he was that age." A shadow came over the widow's face.

Rebecca knew she was remembering her beloved only child, who had died in a hunting accident.

The widow turned to Isaac and said something in Abenaki. He answered her with a few words. Rebecca's eyebrows shot up; she had no idea that the widow knew the Indian language.

Captain Stevens laughed. "I'd forgotten that you and your husband used to trade with the Indians. You remember some of their talk, eh?"

"Enough to get by," said the widow with a small smile. "Rebecca, bring the boy some food."

Rebecca filled a trencher with hot bean soup. She brought it toward the boy reluctantly, noting a strange odor as she came close to him.

He even smells like a savage, she thought.

Isaac grabbed the trencher from her and slurped at the soup. "Ah," the widow said. "It's good to have a boy in the house. Rebecca, be sure to give him cornbread, too."

"We're out of cornbread, ma'am," Rebecca reminded her. "We ate the last at noon."

"Tsk, tsk," the widow clucked. "I'll go over to the Willards and see if I can borrow some." With an air of purpose, the widow made her way out to the Yard.

Left alone with Isaac and Captain Stevens, Rebecca asked the captain eagerly, "Pray, sir, did you hear news of my parents or Benjamin on your mission? Any word at all?"

"No, child," the captain said. His tired face looked sad.

"I inquired many times about your family, but no one knew of them."

"Oh," said Rebecca. She turned away from the captain. She did not want him to see the tears welling in her eyes. *All this time I've hoped and prayed,* she thought. *And still there's nothing.* At last, she burst out, "'Tisn't right! Why should Mama and Papa and Ben still be prisoners when a boy like that"—she jerked her head at Isaac—"a boy who's more Indian than white, is set free!"

"It may not seem right to you," the captain said quietly. "But we must not question God's will. Perhaps one of Isaac's kin wants him back as much as you want your family."

Rebecca looked doubtfully at the savage boy slurping his soup. *How could anyone, anywhere, want him back as much as I want Mama, Papa, and Ben?* she thought.

Suddenly, Isaac looked up from his food. He stared coldly at Rebecca as if he sensed what she was thinking. Rebecca felt a little shiver of fear. She turned to Captain Stevens. "Sir, are you sure he doesn't speak English?"

"He's forgotten all the English he once knew," said Captain Stevens. "It happens when children are taken at a young age. Since he's been with our soldiers, he's learned a few words, like *yes* and *stop*. He knows little more than that."

Isaac now held his empty dish out to Rebecca. He pointed to the pot on the fire.

"I s'pose he has no need for words," Rebecca said. "He makes himself known without 'em." She carried Isaac's dish to the fireplace and filled it half full. Isaac followed behind her. When she turned to hand him his soup, she saw the savage boy rip an apple off the string hanging overhead. He popped the dried ring into his mouth, then began to reach for another.

"No!" Rebecca cried out. "Captain Stevens! Tell him to stop!"

The captain spoke sharply, and Isaac lowered his arm. He took the trencher and returned to his place on the floor.

"I worked hard to put up those apple rings for winter," Rebecca said, glaring at Isaac. "Doesn't he know enough not to eat 'em?"

"He's not used to our ways," the captain said. "He takes what he needs."

Rebecca eyed the boy as if he were a wild—and possibly rabid—dog. "He's a savage!" she exclaimed. "Just like the Indians!"

"No," said Captain Stevens, shaking his head. "I know how you feel about Indians, but they aren't savages. I lived with them a long while, and they taught me much. Their ways are different from ours, Rebecca, but they're people. They're God's creatures, as we are. Don't forget that."

Rebecca avoided the captain's gaze. "Yes, sir," she mumbled.

"I was just about Isaac's age when I was captured by the Abenaki," the captain continued. "Although it's been many years, I still remember the Indians who were cruel to me. But I also remember everyone who offered me kindnesses—a place by their fire, warm moccasins to wear, a piece of bear meat."

He paused, then asked, "How d'ye want to be remembered, Rebecca?"

Before Rebecca could reply, Selinda came through the door. She looked at Rebecca, and her eyes asked silently, *Does the captain have news for us?*

Rebecca shook her head slightly. Selinda bit her lip. Then she curtsied low to Captain Stevens. "Good evening, sir," she said quietly.

"Good evening, Selinda," he replied. "I was reminding your sister that we should treat Isaac the way we ourselves would want to be treated if we were strangers in a strange land."

"We'll do our best, sir," Selinda promised. She smiled shyly at Isaac, but he was busy scraping up the last bits of his soup. "Let me fetch you more," Selinda offered. She limped to the fireplace.

Rebecca noted with dismay that her sister filled the boy's dish all the way to the top. Now there would be little left for their own supper. *Sometimes Selinda is just too good,* she thought to herself.

Captain Stevens stood up from the bench. "I must

leave again tomorrow. I should return by Saturday at the
latest. I trust ye'll be hospitable to Isaac while I am away."

"You leave tomorrow, sir?" Rebecca echoed. *I must ask
for his help now,* she thought. "Pray, sir, may we speak to
you about something?"

Captain Stevens paused, his hand on the door. "Yes?"

"It's about Selinda's contract," Rebecca said. She
quickly explained how Mrs. Cutter was planning to move
back to Connecticut—and take Selinda with her. "She
can't do that, can she, sir?"

"I'm sorry to tell ye," Captain Stevens said, "but if the
Cutters bought Selinda's contract for a year, they're within
their rights to take her. Just as if they'd bought a horse—
they'd have every right to take that with them, too."

"Selinda's not a horse or a slave!" Rebecca exclaimed.
"They didn't buy her!"

"Aye, but when the Cutters bought her indenture, they
bought her services for a period of time—in this case, a
year," Captain Stevens explained. "I know we don't do
indentures much here in the fort, but they're common in
the cities. The only way I've heard of being released from
an indenture before the time is up is to buy the contract
back. Do you have enough money to do that?"

Selinda shook her head sadly. "Mrs. Cutter paid two
pounds for my contract. She says she won't sell it back
for a shilling less."

"All we have now is three shillings," said Rebecca. She

did some quick calculations. There were twenty shillings in a pound, so they would need forty shillings in all. "We need thirty-seven shillings more. The only valuable things we own are the silver spoons." She paused. "Do you remember?"

Captain Stevens nodded. After the girls were rescued, the captain had advised them to keep their spoons hidden and to tell no one about them. "Someday you may need those spoons," he'd told Rebecca. "For now, ye'd best keep them to yourself." Rebecca had followed his instructions carefully, never mentioning the spoons to anyone in the fort.

Now she looked to Captain Stevens again for advice. "Do you think we should sell the spoons — to buy back Selinda's contract?"

"Rebecca, we can't!" Selinda protested. "What would Mama say?"

"What would she say if I let you be taken to Connecticut?" Rebecca asked her sister. She turned to the captain. "What do you think, sir?"

Captain Stevens stroked his graying beard. "I think your mother would believe Selinda is more important than any spoon," he said. "You must do what you need to do, Rebecca. Thirty-seven shillings is a great deal of money for you to raise."

"What's this about thirty-seven shillings?" asked Widow Tyler. The old woman entered the house carrying a basket of cornbread and a jug filled with cider. "The Willards gave me this for our visitor," she said.

She handed Isaac a large chunk of cornbread and a cup of cider. He ate the food greedily. The widow smiled with satisfaction, then turned to Captain Stevens and asked again, "What were you saying about thirty-seven shillings?"

Captain Stevens told the widow about Selinda's dilemma. "'Twould be cruel for the Cutters to take Selinda away!" the widow exclaimed. "But I can't say I'm surprised they're leaving. Amelia Cutter thinks she's too fine for Fort Number 4—her with her boastful ways and fancy dresses!"

The widow patted Selinda's arm. "I wish there was something I could do to help you, dear, but . . ." Her voice trailed off. An awkward silence filled the cabin. Both the Percy sisters and Captain Stevens knew that Widow Tyler did not have a single shilling to spare— much less two pounds.

"Perchance I could speak to Mrs. Cutter," the widow suggested after a moment. "I might persuade her to allow Selinda to stay with us."

Rebecca and Selinda exchanged glances. The widow tended to be more honest than diplomatic, and she and Mrs. Cutter had never been friendly. Any conversation between the two women would be more likely to do harm than good.

Captain Stevens cleared his throat. "That's kind of you, Abigail, but as commander of the fort, I'll speak with Mrs. Cutter."

"Thank you, sir," Rebecca and Selinda replied together. They looked at each other, relieved. Surely Captain Stevens would be able to convince Mrs. Cutter!

The captain said something to Isaac. The boy shrugged and returned to his food. "I told him to help with cutting wood and other chores you might have," Captain Stevens explained. He reached for the door. "Tomorrow, I'll stop in before I leave, and make sure everything is well. Farewell till then."

After the captain left, the room seemed suddenly quiet. Darkness had fallen upon the fort now, and only ashes from the cooking fire lit the cabin. Outside, crickets clicked and frogs gargled their mournful songs. A baby cried in a nearby cabin. Then the sound of its sobbing was replaced by its mother's soothing lullaby.

The widow ate a bowl of the soup, then retired to her bed. Isaac silently retreated to his corner and pulled the curtains closed around the bed. Rebecca divided the small remainder of soup between Selinda and herself, frowning as she did so. She had planned the soup to last two, possibly three days. Now it was gone in a single night.

"Next time you give food to that savage boy, don't serve him so much," Rebecca whispered to her sister.

"You've always said to be kind to guests," Selinda

reminded her. "When Reverend Turner stayed with us last spring, you said we should give him the best of everything."

Rebecca remembered Reverend Turner well. He was a kind man who'd reminded her of Papa. "Reverend Turner was different," Rebecca told her sister. "He was a preacher. Isaac's a savage boy—and he eats like a bear in springtime."

"Maybe Isaac's hungry 'cause the Indians starved him," Selinda suggested.

"Maybe he's just greedy," Rebecca replied. "And if he keeps eating like he did tonight, *we'll* be the ones who'll starve."

Still hungry, the two girls climbed the ladder up to the loft. It was a bare space, not nearly as pleasant as the airy loft they had once shared in their parents' cabin. Their bed was a corn-husk mattress on the floor. Eaves slanted sharply down on either side of the floor. A wooden trunk under the eaves contained their few belongings.

The two girls hung their dresses on nails driven into the rafters, said their prayers, and climbed into bed. As they lay in the darkness together, Selinda said hopefully, "Perhaps 'twill be good to have Isaac here. Captain Stevens said he'd chop wood for us—you know how you hate to do that."

"I don't know if I trust that boy with an ax," Rebecca muttered. "He might think it was a tomahawk and scalp us all."

Selinda was horrified. "Rebecca!" she whispered. "You don't really believe he'd tomahawk us, do you?"

"No," Rebecca admitted. "But I'll keep an eye on him just the same."

Selinda soon fell asleep, but Rebecca lay awake in the darkness and worried. She was finally drifting off when the peaceful night was shattered.

There was a piercing scream, then a cry of "No! Stop! *No!*"

CHAPTER 3

A FIERCE FIGHT

R ebecca bolted upright, her heart pounding hard with the sudden shock of being awakened. In the dim moonlight, she could see Selinda sitting up in bed, her nightclothes wet with sweat. She was shaking all over.

Ever since the raid on their home, Selinda had suffered terrible nightmares. At first, they had tormented her almost every night. Gradually they had become less frequent, but they still haunted Selinda, especially when she was tired or worried.

Rebecca put her arms around her sister and felt her thin ribs heaving. "All is well," Rebecca soothed her. "We're safe."

Selinda began to cry with great, wrenching sobs. Rebecca held her close. "All is well," she repeated. "'Twas a dream."

Suddenly, Rebecca saw a dark head appear at the edge

of the loft. She jumped and almost screamed. Then she
realized it was Isaac. He had climbed partway up the ladder.

"What's wrong?" he demanded.

Rebecca took a deep breath. In the confusion of the
night, she had forgotten about the savage boy downstairs.
"Nothing," she replied. "Go away."

Isaac vanished as quietly as he had appeared. Rebecca
turned back to her sister. "Was it the same dream?" she
asked.

Between sobs, Selinda nodded. "It's as if . . . as if it's
happening all over again," she whispered.

The summer night was warm, but Rebecca felt goose
bumps. She remembered the awful raid all too well. She
also remembered how, for weeks afterward, Selinda had
neither spoken nor cried. She had just sat and stared off
into the distance. Rebecca had fed and dressed her sister,
and she'd tried to protect her from the curiosity of others.
Yet after a few weeks, people had started to say that
Selinda was "not right in the head."

Rebecca had been terrified. She had already lost her
parents and Ben—was she going to lose Selinda, too? She'd
turned to Captain Stevens for advice. He had assured her
that someday Selinda would get better. "She's just mourn-
ing in her own way," he'd said.

The captain had been right. After two months, Selinda
had finally said her first word, *Rebecca*. From then on, her
speech had slowly returned. Yet even now, Selinda often

turned to Rebecca for comfort, especially when the night-mares tore open all her old fears. The girls had a ritual they would go through before returning to sleep, and tonight was no different.

First, Selinda asked her sister whether they had done the right thing by leaving their parents. "Mama told us to go into the cellar," Rebecca assured her sister. "She wanted us to be safe."

"And the spoons?" Selinda asked.

Rebecca usually mentioned the spoons, but tonight she hadn't wanted to. "The spoons are here," Rebecca said. She reached under the mattress and pulled out the small linen pouch that Selinda had sewn for the spoons. Rebecca took the spoons out of their pouch and handed them to her sister. "See?" she said. "They're safe." Selinda touched the cold silver and was reassured.

As Rebecca tucked the precious pouch back under the mattress, she felt an ache of sorrow. She remembered her mother's parting words. "Keep these," Mama had said as she had given her the spoons. "And watch over your sister." *I may not be able to keep the spoons,* Rebecca thought, *but I'll not let the Cutters take away Selinda.*

"Mama, Papa, and Ben *are* going to come back to us someday, aren't they?" Selinda asked, calmer now.

"Of course they're coming home. Mama promised they would." Rebecca always tried to say this in a confident way. Yet she herself worried, *Will they really come back?*

"And you'll never leave me?" Selinda persisted.

"Never," Rebecca replied. "I promise."

At last Selinda was satisfied, and she fell asleep. Rebecca stayed awake. Something was gnawing at her; something was out of place. At last, she realized what it was. As he'd climbed up the ladder, Isaac had said, "What's wrong?"

Isaac does speak English! Rebecca realized. *He's been hiding it. What else is he hiding? And why?*

The next day the girls were up at dawn to do their chores. Rebecca felt tired and irritable. Her mood was not improved by the sound of Isaac snoring in his curtained corner.

It's one thing for the widow to sleep through the morning. She's old and sick, Rebecca thought. *But why should he lie abed?*

She pulled up one of the blankets that curtained Isaac's bed and tied it so it would stay open. "It's morning," she announced briskly. "Time to shake a leg!"

Isaac opened his eyes briefly, then turned over to face the wall.

"Maybe we should let him sleep," Selinda suggested.

"Humph!" Rebecca muttered. She busied herself making their breakfast of cornmeal mush. She worked loudly, banging pots at every opportunity. Then, she had an idea.

She glanced over to Isaac's corner. With a look of horror on her face, she cried out, "Selinda, look! A snake is crawling next to that boy's foot!"

Isaac looked down toward his foot, then abruptly turned back to the wall.

"Where?" Selinda asked, her voice full of concern. "I don't see it!"

"Never mind," Rebecca told her sister. "I was just testing him." She turned toward Isaac. "I know your secret. You do speak English, don't you?"

Isaac ignored her. "Don't you?" Rebecca repeated loudly.

Isaac turned and looked at her, seemingly uncomprehending.

Rebecca stamped her foot. "Don't play the fool," she said. "I heard you last night. You said, 'What's wrong?'"

Isaac lifted himself up on one elbow. "Whatswrong? Whatswrong? Whatswrong?" he demanded in a singsong voice. "Yes. No. Stop. Go. Water. Horse." He pointed to the fireplace. "Fire, food. Speak English, yes? No."

"I think he only knows a few words," Selinda whispered.

"I think he's pretending," Rebecca said loudly. "He knew what I was saying about the snake."

She gestured toward Isaac. "Why should you lie abed while we do all the work?" she demanded. "You heard

Widow Tyler last night—we need some wood chopped."

Isaac did not respond.

Rebecca swung an imaginary ax in the air. "CHOP—THE—WOOD!" she said slowly and loudly. She unbarred the back window and pointed to the woodpile that stood in the grassy space between the back of the house and the palisade. "Out there!"

Still, Isaac lay motionless.

Selinda stepped forward. "He doesn't understand, Becca," she said softly. She picked up the ax by the door. "I'll chop the wood. I'm big enough now, and I've a little time before the Cutters'll be expecting me."

Before Rebecca could protest, Selinda unbarred the back door and limped outside with the ax, which was almost as tall as she was. From the back window, Rebecca watched her sister try to split a heavy log. *Thud!* The ax fell dully on the hard wood, barely nicking the surface. Selinda pulled out the ax and tried again. And again. The blade bounced off the wood.

"Of all the foolishness!" Rebecca said finally. "I s'pose I must do it myself."

She started out the door to help Selinda, but Isaac, without a word, stood up and brushed her aside. He walked out to the woodpile and took the ax from Selinda. Then he swung it high into the air. *Crack! Crack!* With strong, sure strokes, he split the wood into quarters.

As Isaac reached for another log, Selinda began to

speak to him. Rebecca could not hear what her sister was saying, but she could guess. From the doorway, she watched Selinda gesture with her hands, first reaching tall, then holding her hand a little above her head, then finally pointing down to the height of a small child. Isaac listened carefully but without expression. Then he shook his head. Selinda limped back toward Rebecca.

"I asked him if he'd ever met a man named Josiah Percy, a woman named Martha Percy, or a little boy called Benjamin," Selinda said.

"Did he say anything?" asked Rebecca.

Selinda shook her head sadly.

"I'm not sure he'd have told us even if he *did* know something," Rebecca said. "I think he likes Indians more than white people."

"Don't be too hard on him," Selinda said. "He's not been with us long."

"Why are you taking his side?" Rebecca demanded. "Have you forgotten what the Indians did to us?" As soon as the words were out of her mouth, Rebecca regretted them. She knew Selinda could never forget the raid—any more than she herself could. But why did Selinda have to be so confounded kind to the savage boy?

Selinda hung her head. "I'd never forget the raid, Becca. But Isaac had naught to do with that. And I think of Ben and how I'd want someone to be to him if he was freed from the Indians as Isaac was. Besides," and now she looked up at her sister, "he did come out and help me with the wood."

"Seems to me it was his job to start with," Rebecca said shortly. She turned and walked back into the house.

Isaac continued to work on the log pile as the sisters finished their chores. When Widow Tyler woke up, she had a coughing spell. Rebecca made her tea with honey to soothe her throat. The widow drank it gratefully. Then she asked, "Where's the boy?"

Rebecca explained that Isaac was chopping wood. Widow Tyler smiled. "I knew he'd be a help to us," she said, and then she was caught by another spasm of coughing. Rebecca poured more hot water into her tea and gave her the last spoonful of honey from the crock.

"That's the end of the honey, ma'am," she told the widow. "I'm sorry."

"'Tis a shame," said the widow. Both she and Rebecca knew there was no money to spend on a luxury like honey. The widow sighed. "Well, perhaps God will provide."

The widow sat in her chair and read her Bible until her head began to nod. Then she returned to bed for a nap. The sun was fully up now, and all the settlers were beginning their day's work. Before leaving for the Cutters, Selinda carried a cup of water out to Isaac.

"'Twill soon be hot out," Selinda explained to her sister. "And Isaac is working hard."

Rebecca glanced outside. A pile of cut logs was growing

next to Isaac. "He's doing well enough, I daresay," she said grudgingly. "I hope he stacks those logs, too."

Soon after Selinda left, Rebecca was startled by a man's hoarse singing:

"Mend and fix,
Trade and sell,
I do it all,
And I do it well!"

It was the peddler, Old Johnny. He was going from cabin to cabin advertising his wares. Now he stood in the doorway of the widow's cabin, his leather bag slung over his shoulder.

"What say ye, young lady?" Johnny asked. "Any pots need mending? Anything to buy or sell? I've some lovely cloth here and buttons of all kinds."

Rebecca swallowed hard. She had been thinking about how she could sell the spoons. Few people at Fort Number 4 had money for a luxury like silver. But the peddler traveled to many settlements. Surely he would know someone who could afford the beautiful spoons.

Nervously, she wiped her hands on her apron, then curtsied politely. "Yes, sir, we may have some things for sale. Do you buy silver spoons?"

Just then Ezekiel Cutter walked up behind the peddler. "Silver!" Ezekiel jeered. "Hah! What's a girl like you know about silver? I s'pose you've a gold crown, too, eh?"

Rebecca drew herself up. "The Cutters aren't the only family in this fort with fine things," she said. "Besides, Ezekiel, I wasn't talking to you, was I?"

Ezekiel touched his hat mockingly. "Well, excuse me, Miss Fine Lady. I didn't want to talk with you neither." He looked over the peddler's head and peered into the widow's dark cabin. "Where's that Indian boy? He's the one I'm looking for."

"He's out back, at the woodpile," Rebecca told him. Ezekiel left, and she turned to the peddler. "Pray, sir, come inside," she said. She pointed toward the curtained area where the widow's bed stood. "Widow Tyler's asleep, but she won't hear us if we're quiet."

Old Johnny walked inside the cabin with the silent steps of a man who had spent a long time in the wilderness. His quick gray eyes took in the corner bed where Isaac had slept. "Too bad that boy is staying here with you," he said in a low tone. "Watch out for him."

"What do you mean?"

The peddler took a seat on the bench. "I've seen white children who've been raised by Indians. Sometimes, if they're ransomed and brought back to their own kin, it works all right. They're glad to be back home. But more often . . ." he let his voice trail off.

"What happens?" Rebecca asked anxiously.

"Well, most often the young'uns, specially the boys,

don't want to come back at all," Johnny explained.
"They've grown used to the Indian ways, and they want
to stay with their tribe—no matter how much their white
kin cry, carry on, and beg 'em to come back."

Rebecca nodded. She'd heard of captives who, after
years of living with the Indians, had refused to return to
their white families. But she had never understood it.

"The Indians hate us as much as we hate them, don't
they?" she asked the peddler. "Why do they want to adopt
white children?"

Johnny shrugged. "Many Indians have died of sickness,
and they need more people for their tribes. The way they
see it, once they've had their ceremonies and all, the white
young'uns are as good as blood kin to them."

Rebecca looked down at the scarred wooden table. It
was terrible to think of a white child brought up by Indians.
Are Mama and Papa still alive? she wondered. *And what has
become of Benjamin? Does he now call some Indian woman
"mama"?* She shuddered at the thought.

"The young'uns come to think of themselves as
Indians," the peddler continued. "And if they're forced
to come back and live with white folks, ofttimes they
become thieving no-goods, just like the Indians. So you
watch out for that boy Isaac, you hear?"

"I will," Rebecca promised.

The peddler leaned back on the bench. "Well, then,
you talked about some silver you wanted to sell?"

"Aye," said Rebecca. She paused, then spoke as if the words were pulled out of her. "Could you tell me, perhaps, how much a silver spoon would sell for?"

Johnny's eyes narrowed. "How many spoons d'ye have — and what do they look like?"

"Two spoons, each about so long," Rebecca said, spreading her hands about six inches apart, "with designs at the bottom."

"Spoons such as that might fetch as much as thirteen, maybe fourteen shillings each," Johnny said slowly. "Of course, I'd have to look at 'em."

Rebecca rose from the table and headed for the ladder that led to the loft. "I'll fetch them —" she began. She was interrupted by a shout from outside. It sounded as if it came from the woodpile. Rebecca hurried to the window. She was horrified to see that Isaac had taken off his shirt and was now bare from the waist up.

"Pardon me, sir, I must go," she told the peddler. "I'll show you the spoons later." She rushed out to the wood-pile. Children from some neighboring families had gathered in the grassy area behind the houses. They were pointing at Isaac, and the girls were giggling at the sight of a half-naked white boy.

Ezekiel Cutter stood next to the woodpile. "Hey!" he taunted Isaac. "Don't you have enough sense to wear clothes?"

Isaac continued to chop wood.

Ezekiel leaned down and picked up a chunk of wood the size of a brick. "You listen when I talk!" he demanded. He threw the wood chunk hard at Isaac's head. Isaac dodged, but the wood nicked his ear. A trickle of blood ran down his neck.

Isaac turned and hurled down his ax. With a sudden, swift movement, he threw himself at Ezekiel, knocking the bigger boy off his feet. They grappled on the ground, first with Isaac on top, then Ezekiel, then Isaac again. Then Ezekiel, using all his strength, threw Isaac off and scrambled to his feet.

Ezekiel pulled out the long knife he always wore by his side. It had a white bone handle into which he had carved the letters *E.C.* Holding the blade out, he taunted, "How do you like this knife, Indian boy? Want to come get it?"

Rebecca drew a sharp breath. Isaac was unarmed. It wasn't fair. "Stop!" she cried out. No one paid attention to her.

Isaac rose to his feet, his face still expressionless, his eyes focused on Ezekiel. For a few moments, the boys circled each other. Then Ezekiel saw an opening. He lunged toward Isaac. Isaac stepped back just in time. With a powerful kick to Ezekiel's arm, he sent the knife flying.

Now both boys were unarmed. Isaac closed in on Ezekiel, wrestling him to the ground. Ezekiel fought hard, but Isaac attacked harder. Rebecca stared in amazement. She had seen boys fight before, but never so fiercely. And no boy in the fort had ever beaten Ezekiel Cutter.

Isaac's no coward, she thought with grudging respect.

Finally, Isaac pinned the bigger boy to the ground. It was clear he'd won. But instead of releasing Ezekiel, Isaac grabbed him by the shoulders. Then he started beating Ezekiel's head into the hard-packed ground.

A terrifying realization flashed through Rebecca's mind. *That savage is going to kill Ezekiel!*

CHAPTER 4

BOUND BY LAW

S top!" roared Captain Stevens,
striding across the grass. He yelled
something in Abenaki. Isaac pulled
himself off the older boy and stood up.
"What happened?" Captain Stevens
asked angrily.

"That savage just came at me!"
Ezekiel charged. "I wasn't doing nothing."

Captain Stevens looked around at the group of children clustered near the woodpile. News of the fight had traveled fast in the small fort, and more than a dozen children had now gathered in the grassy area. Rebecca saw her sister among the group. Selinda looked pale and worried.

"Is that true?" Captain Stevens asked the assembled children. A few minutes before, several of the boys had been cheering loudly for Ezekiel. Now the whole group was silent under Captain Stevens' stern eye.

"Did Isaac start the fight?" the captain demanded.

Rebecca hesitated, but Selinda stepped forward. "No," she said quietly. "Ezekiel started it."

Captain Stevens looked at Ezekiel, who was bloody from the pounding he'd received. "I hope you learned a lesson," he told the redheaded boy. Then the captain said something in Abenaki. Isaac picked up his shirt and stalked back to Widow Tyler's cabin.

The captain watched Isaac go. Then he turned to the assembled children. "I'm leaving the fort now, but I'll be back in a few days. There shall be no trouble while I'm gone, do ye understand?"

Everyone nodded. Ezekiel looked down at his feet.

"If anyone starts another fight, he'll be seriously punished. I'll see to it myself," the captain continued. He looked through the palisade to the dark, forested hills beyond the fort. "We have enemies all around us. We don't need to be fighting among ourselves, too."

The captain turned away and headed toward Widow Tyler's back door. He let himself in, strode quickly through the cabin, and then walked out the front door into the Yard. Rebecca hurried after him. As she passed through the cabin, she saw that the widow was still asleep and that Isaac had pulled the curtains shut around his bed.

"Captain Stevens!" Rebecca called when she reached the Yard, but the fort's commander was so wrapped up in his own thoughts that he didn't hear her. He had just

reached the South Gate when Rebecca caught up to him.
"Excuse me, sir, did you speak with Mrs. Cutter?"

"Aye, I'd come to the widow's cabin to tell you about
it, but then I saw the fight," the captain said, frowning.
"Mrs. Cutter's determined to leave—and take your sister
with her."

"She can't!"

"She is within her rights," Captain Stevens replied
sternly. Then he looked in Rebecca's eyes, and his tone softened. "I must go now, but I'll try to talk with Mrs. Cutter
again when I return."

That may be too late! Rebecca wanted to cry out. But
the words choked in her throat. "Yes, sir," she said.

The sentry opened the South Gate, and Rebecca saw
five of Captain Stevens' men assembled on horseback
just outside the fort. One of the men held Scoggin, the
captain's horse. The captain jumped on Scoggin and rode
away with his men.

As the gate closed behind the men, Rebecca felt very
much alone. She walked slowly back toward Widow Tyler's
cabin.

She found Ezekiel and Selinda standing in front of
the cabin. Ezekiel was glaring down at the younger girl.
"You had to defend that Indian, didn't you?" he accused
her. "You'll see where that gets you."

"Don't you threaten my sister!" Rebecca burst out.
"Or I'll—"

"Or you'll what?" Ezekiel asked. He wiped his blood-stained face. "Your sister belongs to my family now." He turned to Selinda. "Get back to our house! After I wash up, I'll tell my mother how you lied and made trouble for me."

Rebecca watched forlornly as Selinda followed Ezekiel back across the Yard. Selinda entered the Cutters' cabin, but Ezekiel went to the well to wash the blood and dirt off his face.

I must talk to Mrs. Cutter, Rebecca decided. *And I'd better do it now, before Ezekiel poisons her mind against us.* She took a deep breath. She dreaded the thought of calling on Mrs. Cutter, but she remembered how her father used to say, "Do the worst job first, then the rest will all seem easy." She forced herself to cross the Yard and knock at the Cutters' door. Mrs. Cutter opened it a crack. She was a tall woman with cold blue eyes and a jutting chin like her son's.

"Begging your pardon, ma'am, may I speak to you?" Rebecca asked.

"If it's about Selinda, you're wasting your time," Mrs. Cutter said sharply. "As I told Captain Stevens, a contract is a contract. I've paid for a full year of Selinda's labor, and she will come with us."

Rebecca's hopes sank, yet she continued. "Please, ma'am, may I come in, just for a moment?"

Mrs. Cutter opened the door. "Very well, but only for a moment. I have much to do."

Rebecca followed Mrs. Cutter inside. The cabin smelled of lye soap, and damp dresses and bedcovers hung from the rafters. A dozen or more brightly colored hair ribbons, all freshly washed, fluttered in the breeze by the window. Selinda was in the corner, pinning a dress onto Priscilla Cutter. The material was colored the bright blue of a robin's egg, and the dress was cut in the style all the ladies in Boston were wearing. Selinda smiled up at her sister, her mouth filled with pins.

Mrs. Cutter frowned. "Selinda, go outside and turn the quilts. See that they dry evenly."

"Selinda must finish this dress, Mama," Priscilla complained, "or I shall have nothing to wear in Connecticut!"

"She will finish it later, dear," Mrs. Cutter said firmly. "Selinda, do as I say. I want to speak to your sister in private."

As soon as Selinda left, Mrs. Cutter turned toward Rebecca. "Well?"

"Ma'am," Rebecca blurted out, "please don't take Selinda with you!" She explained to Mrs. Cutter how important it was that she and Selinda stay together. "Since our parents and Benjamin were taken, all we've had is each other."

"A contract is a contract," Mrs. Cutter repeated briskly. "If you cannot buy back your sister's contract, you must accept that she is leaving with us."

Rebecca felt her anger rising, but she forced herself

to ask humbly, "If Selinda must go with you, then may I come, too? I'd be sorry to leave Widow Tyler, but I'd go if it meant that Selinda and I would not be parted." Rebecca saw a glimmer of interest in Mrs. Cutter's eyes when she added, "I'd work for free. All I'd need is bed and board."

Before Mrs. Cutter could answer, Ezekiel walked into the house. His face was clean now, but a fresh bruise blackened his forehead. "Don't listen to her, Mother," he declared. "She wants to make trouble."

Mrs. Cutter scowled at her son. "What happened to you?"

"The savage boy attacked me," Ezekiel claimed, with a look of injured innocence. "And she," he pointed at Rebecca, "and her sister told Captain Stevens that it was my fault."

"That's not true!" Rebecca protested.

Mrs. Cutter eyed Rebecca disapprovingly. "It's clear you're a bad influence on Selinda. She'll be better off without you. In fact, I'm probably doing her a favor by taking her with us."

Rebecca's anger burst out. "Doing her a favor!" she exclaimed. She gestured at the finery hanging about the house. "You don't give a fig about my sister. All you care about are dresses and hair ribbons, and what styles Selinda can sew for you!"

"Your sister is coming with me whether you like it

or not," Mrs. Cutter said icily. She pointed at the door. "Now leave this house—and don't come back!"

Rebecca walked slowly across the dusty Yard back to the widow's house. When she entered the cabin, she saw Isaac sitting cross-legged on his bed. He was whittling a heavy stick with a knife that had once belonged to Widow Tyler's husband. Usually, the knife hung by the fireplace. Rebecca was annoyed that Isaac had taken it down. *He just helps himself to whatever he wants,* she thought.

She turned on the savage boy. "Why did you fight with Ezekiel? Selinda works for his family. You've made things worse for her."

Isaac looked up from his whittling. "He fight." He paused and touched his ear. It was still bloody. "Me fight."

Rebecca knew he was right. Ezekiel had started the fight; Isaac had only defended himself. But she was still angry. "You didn't have to beat him that hard," she persisted. "You could've killed him."

Isaac did not reply. He returned to his whittling. Rebecca was sure that this savage boy understood much more English than he admitted. "Killed," she repeated loudly. "You could have killed him!"

"No kill," Isaac said quietly. Suddenly, he drew back his arm. With a flick of his wrist he sent the hunting knife sailing across the room. It skewered an apple ring, then dug itself deeply into a rafter of the ceiling.

Isaac stood up and retrieved the knife. Then he returned to his seat on the bed and picked up his whittling again. He expertly shaved a thin white slice of wood from the heavy stick in his hands. Rebecca stared at him, and he looked up at her, his eyes tight, angry slits. "No kill," he repeated.

Rebecca felt a cold twist of fear in her stomach. *He's telling me that he could have killed Ezekiel, but he chose not to,* she realized. *I wonder if he hates us all.*

CHAPTER 5

MISSING

A few hours later, Rebecca stood in line at one of the wells in the Yard. The sun beat down on her linen cap, and the back of her dress was damp with sweat. A wooden yoke sat heavily on her shoulders, and empty pails dangled from either side of it. As she waited for her turn to draw water, she looked around the Yard, hoping to catch sight of Old Johnny. She had not seen him since she'd had to rush out to the woodpile, and she needed to talk with him about the spoons.

"Good day, Rebecca!" a cheerful voice behind her exclaimed. "'Tis hot as an oven on baking day, isn't it?"

Rebecca turned around and saw that thirteen-year-old Hannah Randolph had joined the line behind her. Hannah's parents were the fort's shopkeepers. They kept supplies of flour, molasses, salt, and other necessities in a corner of their cabin and traded with other settlers.

Hannah was a friendly, talkative girl who always knew
the latest gossip.

Now she fanned herself with one hand and asked
Rebecca curiously, "What's the white Indian boy like?
Is it true he doesn't talk?"

"It's true," Rebecca told her. "Folks have been coming
by and asking him questions about friends or kin who've
been captured. He says naught to them—just sits there
and whittles."

"Ooh!" Hannah exclaimed with a shudder. "I don't
know how you stand it. I'd hate being in the same house
with an Indian—even if he were white. Indians give me
the shakes!"

If only you knew how much they scare me, Rebecca thought.
But all she said was, "Aye, me too."

It was now Rebecca's turn to draw water. First, she
filled one of her buckets, then she began the next. As
Rebecca worked, Hannah chattered on. "Miriam Willard
was here not long ago. She was telling everybody about
the party that the Johnsons are having out at their farm
Friday night."

Rebecca nodded. Miriam was the daughter of the
fort's second-in-command, Lieutenant Moses Willard.
She lived with her sister and brother-in-law, Susanna and
James Johnson, on the Johnsons' farm just outside the
fort. Miriam helped her sister take care of the Johnsons'
three children—little Susanna, Sylvanus, and Polly.

"The Johnsons are inviting everyone to their party,"
Hannah continued. "I can hardly wait. I haven't danced
in ages! You'll be going, won't you?"

"I think not," said Rebecca. She hung her filled buckets onto the wooden yoke. The two buckets balanced each
other, making the heavy load easier to carry. "We have
no one to escort us from the fort."

"You must come!" Hannah urged. "'Twill be merry
if many of us dance together! You and Selinda could walk
with my family."

"Thank you," said Rebecca. She was pleased to be
invited, but the mention of Selinda reminded her of how
desperately she needed to see Old Johnny. "Have you
perchance seen the peddler?"

"Indeed I have," Hannah reported. "He rode out
of the fort about noon. I heard him tell the sentry he'd
be back by sunset." Her eyes narrowed curiously. "Have
you something to buy—or sell? My mama's been buying
needlework lately. Is that what you have?"

Rebecca knew her friend's fondness for gossip, so
she answered vaguely. "Oh, aye, a few odds and ends."
Water sloshed from the buckets as she started walking
away, carefully balancing the yoke on her shoulders.
"Good day, Hannah!"

Rebecca returned home and busied herself with
her chores, trying to stay as far away from Isaac as she
could. At midafternoon, there was a knock on the door.

When she opened the door, she was surprised to see Private Chandler. He was carrying a bucket with a chunk of lye soap in it.

"Before he left, Captain Stevens told me to take Isaac down to the river today for a washing," the private explained. "It'll be his first step back to living like white folks."

The widow cupped her hand over her ear. "Eh?"

Private Chandler repeated his message loudly. "Can't he go on his own?" the widow asked. "He's a big boy— he doesn't need you to watch over him."

Private Chandler shook his head. "Orders are he's not to leave the fort without a guard. The captain don't want him runnin' back to the Indians."

"Where would he go?" the widow scoffed. She looked out the window. Fort Number 4 was rimmed by mountains and forests on three sides and by the river on the fourth side. "'Tis a long journey back to where he came from. How would an unarmed boy get there by himself— specially with the first frosts not far away?"

Private Chandler stood stiffly. "I have my orders, ma'am."

The widow sighed. "Very well," she said. She spoke to Isaac in Abenaki and mimicked the action of washing. Isaac gave the widow a long look, as if he wondered whether to agree to her request. Then he silently rose to his feet.

"Wait," said the widow. She made her way over to her

trunk and pulled out a man's shirt and breeches. "These belonged to my Ethan," she told Private Chandler. "Give 'em to Isaac after he's washed."

Private Chandler left with Isaac, and Rebecca was relieved to have the savage boy gone. She washed dishes, tidied the cabin, then set to work pickling the cucumbers.

She began by draining away the salty water in which the cucumbers had been soaking. Then she rinsed the cucumbers in fresh water, dried them, and put them in crocks. Next, she filled the widow's biggest pot with vinegar and put it over the fire. As the pot heated, the sharp smell of vinegar filled the cabin. Rebecca held her nose as she stirred herbs into the pot.

When the mixture finally came to a boil, she ladled the scalding liquid into the crocks filled with cucumbers. Then she carried the crocks outside to cool in the shade of the cabin. *Now we'll have something to eat with our beans in the winter,* she thought with satisfaction.

She went back to the well to draw more water for the evening meal. Several other women and girls were already waiting in line with their buckets, so Rebecca had to stand in the hot sun for what seemed like forever. While she waited, she kept an eye out for the peddler, but he did not appear.

When she finally returned to Widow Tyler's cabin, Rebecca was surprised to see Ezekiel walking out the front door. He looked nervous, and when he saw Rebecca he stopped. "Where's that boy?" he asked.

"He's not here," Rebecca replied. She noticed that the bruise on Ezekiel's forehead had grown bigger and darker. "You should stay away from him."

"Hah!" Ezekiel muttered. "I can care for myself." He strode away.

Rebecca entered the house. The widow was asleep. Rebecca doubted that she'd even been aware of Ezekiel's visit. *What is Ezekiel up to?* Rebecca wondered. *I hope he leaves us alone.*

Soon Private Chandler was knocking at the door again. When Rebecca opened it, she saw a young man standing behind the private. For a moment, she wondered who the stranger was. Then she realized—it was Isaac.

Ethan's old clothes fit Isaac as if they had been made for him. His hair, which had been greasy, was now a clean, light brown. It was tied back with a strip of leather, and for the first time, Rebecca could clearly see Isaac's face. He had green eyes, high cheekbones, and a strong mouth. *He's not bad looking,* she thought. *He might even be handsome, if he ever smiled.*

Private Chandler grinned. "Cleaned up good, didn't he?"

The widow, awakened by the knock, approached the doorway. Her eyes held a faraway look, and Rebecca wondered whether she was remembering the son who had once worn those clothes.

"And there's something else," the private continued.

"On our way back from the river, we took the north route, past your old farm, Rebecca. Do you remember the big elm tree?"

Rebecca nodded. The Percys' cabin was now a burned ruin surrounded by overgrown fields, but there was still a giant elm in the corner of the yard. It was close to Fairyland, and Rebecca and Selinda had often played under its branches.

"We was passing by that tree and Isaac spied a beehive," Private Chandler said. "Well, I tell you, he can climb faster than a squirrel. He shimmied up that tree, and he grabbed this." Private Chandler held out a large piece of honeycomb wrapped in a handkerchief. "Didn't get stung or nothing. Guess all the bees had moved somewhere else."

"Honey!" The widow exclaimed. Her eyes shone with happiness. "I knew the Lord would provide. Isn't it wonderful, Rebecca?"

"Yes, ma'am," Rebecca said, but she wished Isaac had never set foot on her family's farm—even to get a honeycomb.

Widow Tyler gratefully took the honeycomb from Private Chandler and spoke in Abenaki to Isaac. He nodded and came into the house. He sat down on his bed and began whittling as if there were no one else in the room.

Soon Selinda came home. She was later than usual, and she looked tired. She brightened when she saw Isaac in his clean, new clothes, and she was thrilled by the honeycomb he had found. Then Isaac handed her what he had whittled: a walking stick that fit Selinda perfectly.

"'Tis very kind of you!" she exclaimed. She took a few steps with the aid of the stick. "It eases my walking greatly!"

Rebecca was pleased to see both her sister and the widow smiling. *Perhaps I've been too hasty in my judgment of Isaac,* she thought grudgingly.

That night Isaac again had several helpings of supper—with liberal lacings of honey on his cornbread. *I wonder if he brought the honey because he wanted to be kind?* Rebecca thought as she watched him lick the sticky golden syrup off his fingers. *Or was it only because he wanted something sweet?*

Isaac glanced up and saw Rebecca watching him. He glared at her, then pulled off the leather strip that tied back his hair. His hair fell forward, shielding his face once again. Then he rose from the table and, without a word, returned to his bed, closing the curtains after himself.

All he wants to do is sleep—and eat all our food, Rebecca thought resentfully. After supper was over, she washed the dishes, then measured out dried beans to soak for the next day's dinner. She looked at the remaining beans in the barrel, then called to the widow, in a voice loud enough for Isaac to hear, "Ma'am, we'll run out of beans soon if that boy keeps eating so much."

The widow frowned slightly. "I suppose we'll have to buy more from Mrs. Randolph. Still, it does my heart good to have a boy in the house again." She rose from her chair. "Good night, girls. Sleep well."

As the two sisters prepared for bed, Rebecca told her sister about her meeting with Old Johnny. "I talked to him about our spoons. He seemed interested in buying them. He said he'd have to see 'em before he offers us a price, but he thought they'd be worth thirteen, maybe fourteen shillings each."

Selinda added the sums in her head. Then she looked up at her sister, her forehead creased with worry. "That wouldn't be enough money! We need forty shillings in all!"

"We must bargain with him, the way that Mama and Papa always did," Rebecca resolved. "Papa used to say that no one ever takes the first price they're offered, and we won't either."

"But what if it's not enough?" Selinda asked. "What if we're a few shillings short, and Mrs. Cutter says I still must go with them?"

"There must be other things we could sell," Rebecca assured her. "Let's look."

The girls opened their trunk. By the dim light of the moon through the loft window, they sorted through the trunk's musty contents. The only clothes they had were castoffs from other settlers. For winter, each girl had a heavy shawl, as well as mittens, extra petticoats, and thick woolen underclothes.

"None of these would sell for much," said Rebecca as

she looked through the patched and worn winter clothing. "Besides, it'll be cold before long."

The trunk also contained a heavy box of iron nails that had been salvaged from their burned cabin and barn. Rebecca and Selinda had kept the nails carefully stored in hopes that Papa would someday use them to build a new house.

"We could sell the nails," Rebecca told her sister. "Papa could get new ones when he comes back." *If he comes back,* she thought sadly.

Selinda pulled out a woolen quilt she had made from scraps of worn-out blankets. "Perhaps we could sell this." The girls looked at each other. If they sold this quilt, they would have only one wool quilt to keep them warm over the freezing New Hampshire winter. But they would still have each other . . .

"Very well," Rebecca agreed. "We'll sell the quilt, too, if we must." Rebecca reached for her sister's hand. It was callused and pricked from too many hours of sewing. "But perhaps we won't need to."

The two sisters went to bed. Rebecca was tired, and soon she was sleeping soundly. In the middle of the night, however, she was awakened again by a sharp cry. "No!" Selinda called out despairingly. "No!"

"Shhhhh! All is well," Rebecca whispered. She was relieved when Selinda did not awaken fully but instead fell back into a deep sleep.

Rebecca lay in the darkness. She tried to get back to sleep herself, but the sleeping loft was hot, and she was thirsty. Her tongue felt like sheep's wool. What she wouldn't give for a dipperful of water . . .

She quietly eased herself out of bed and, careful not to wake Selinda, climbed down the ladder and helped herself to a drink. It was cooler downstairs, and the water felt good on her throat. Standing in the quiet cabin, she listened to the sounds of the night. Mosquitoes whined, and a fly buzzed aimlessly. The widow coughed, then resumed her raspy breathing. Upstairs, Selinda shifted on the mattress.

Everyone's asleep, Rebecca thought. Then she realized that no sounds were coming from behind Isaac's curtains. She listened hard, but there was nothing. *Do Indians even sleep quietly?* she wondered.

Curiosity overcame Rebecca. She tiptoed to the edge of Isaac's curtained space, held her breath, and listened as intently as she could. There was not a single sound. Carefully, she picked up a corner of one of the curtains.

By the dim moonlight she could see the bed. The covers were rumpled. But the savage boy was gone!

CHAPTER 6

A THIEF

As Rebecca stood beside the empty bed, she heard footsteps outside. Was it Isaac? If so, what would he think if he caught her downstairs spying on him? Quickly, Rebecca climbed the ladder and slid back into bed beside Selinda.

But the footsteps passed by Widow Tyler's cabin. Rebecca realized it must have been the guard making his rounds. She lay in the darkness, listening for Isaac's return, but the only sound from the room below was the widow coughing in her sleep.

Where can he be? Rebecca worried. The widow's front door opened into the fort's Yard. The only exit from the Yard was through the guarded South Gate, and Rebecca knew that the soldiers would never allow Isaac to leave in the middle of the night. If Isaac had left by the front door, he must still be somewhere inside the fort's Yard.

Perhaps he was thirsty, like me, Rebecca thought.

Mayhap he's gone to get a dipper of water from the well.

Rebecca continued to wait. As time passed, she realized Isaac had to be doing more than getting a drink of water. She imagined the savage boy alone inside the fort, perhaps hiding in the shadows so the guards would not spy him. She remembered vividly how Mrs. Randolph had told her husband, "I wouldn't sleep easy with a boy like that in our house. I'd be afraid he'd attack us in the night."

Would Isaac attack us? Rebecca wondered. She recalled how he had thrown the knife that morning. With a flick of the wrist, he had plunged the blade into the wooden rafter. "No kill," he'd said. But had he really meant "No kill—yet"?

She tried to shake off that thought. She remembered how clean and neat Isaac had looked when he'd returned from his bath in the river. She also remembered Selinda's smile when he had wordlessly given her the walking stick. *He's not all bad,* Rebecca thought. *Perhaps he decided to walk outside where the air is cooler—but wouldn't the guards have stopped him?*

Rebecca wished she'd thought to check the back door, which led to the grassy area between the houses and the palisade. The back door was always barred from the inside at night, but Isaac could have easily unbarred it, and the widow never would have heard him leave.

Could Isaac have gone to the outhouse? Rebecca wondered. Then another possibility occurred to her, and her stomach clenched with worry. *Or could he have escaped the palisade?*

The back area was completely encircled by the palisade, but over time some of the huge logs had shifted a bit. Rebecca knew that in the northwest corner of the fort, children, especially thin ones, could slide between the logs. She had tried it once herself a few years ago, when sneaking into the fort had seemed like an exciting thing to do. A guard had caught her, and she'd been sternly lectured.

Now she wondered if Isaac had slipped through the palisade. Would he try to run back to the Indians? If he found his tribe, would he encourage them to attack the fort? He knew all about the fort's defenses now . . .

Dozens of possibilities whirled through Rebecca's mind. She wished she knew how long the savage boy had been gone—then she would know better what to do. She lay in bed next to Selinda and listened to her sister's breathing. *Surely he could not be in the outhouse this long,* Rebecca decided at last. *I must tell the guards that he's missing.*

Then she heard a creaking noise downstairs and felt a rush of fresh air. A door had opened. She guessed it was the back door, but she couldn't be sure. There was a tiny thump as the door closed again. Rebecca heard the creak of Isaac settling into his bed. Then the cabin was quiet again.

Where has he been? Rebecca wondered as she began to drift back to sleep. *And how long was he gone?*

In the morning, Rebecca told her sister about Isaac's mysterious disappearance.

"Mayhap he had a stomachache," Selinda said. "He did eat a great deal. And beans, well . . ." She laughed a little, embarrassed by what she'd suggested. "Perhaps he's never used a chamber pot. He might've spent much of the night in the outhouse."

Rebecca smiled. "Mayhap," she agreed. "And perhaps he won't be such a hog today."

The girls did their morning chores together before Selinda left for the Cutters. Widow Tyler ate breakfast, then announced she would pay a visit to Mrs. Randolph and try to trade some old needlework she had for more beans and cornmeal. Rebecca was left with only Isaac, who snored in his corner.

There was a loud knocking at the door. Rebecca opened it to discover Private Chandler accompanied by Ezekiel and Priscilla Cutter.

"I must search your house," the private said. He looked uncomfortable. "Ezekiel says his knife's missing. He's sure Isaac took it."

"That's right!" Ezekiel said hotly. He pointed at Isaac, who had awakened and was now standing by his bed. "He tried to get my knife yesterday when we was fighting. When he couldn't get it fair and square, he stole it!"

That was not the way Rebecca remembered the fight. But she thought back to the previous night, when Isaac had been missing. "Did you see him take it?" she asked Ezekiel.

"Nay," he admitted. "But when I got up this morning it was gone. He must've snuck into our house and stolen it. Them Indians'll steal anything!"

Priscilla Cutter stepped forward, her yellow curls bouncing. She looked up appealingly at the young private. "My brother has been wronged by this savage boy!" she said, pointing at Isaac. "It's up to you to do your duty, Private Chandler."

Private Chandler drew himself up. "Very well," he agreed. Despite Rebecca's protests, he began to search the cabin. Ezekiel urged him to pay special attention to Isaac's sleeping area. Together, Ezekiel and the private tore apart the trundle bed where Isaac slept. They separated the feather bed mattress from the corn-husk mattress and patted each thoroughly. Feathers burst from the mattress, but they did not find a hidden knife.

Isaac watched without expression as his clothes and few possessions were searched. Then he began whittling.

"Would that be the knife we're looking for?" the private asked, gesturing at the knife in Isaac's hand.

"That's the widow's knife," Rebecca told him.

Selinda entered the house quietly. She carried her new walking stick, and she spoke up in Isaac's defense. "Isaac can use the widow's knife whenever he wants. Why would he steal another one?"

Ezekiel glared at her. "Be quiet!"

"Well," Private Chandler reported at last, "I don't see your knife."

"It must be here!" Ezekiel exclaimed. He looked surprised.

"Maybe it's upstairs," Priscilla suggested. She led the way up the ladder to the loft, with Rebecca close behind her. Private Chandler looked through the girls' few belongings in the trunk. Then he checked their bed. Rebecca knew that in a moment he would uncover their precious spoons.

"Leave our things alone!" she protested. But the private had already picked up the mattress and was looking underneath. Rebecca shut her eyes, dreading the moment when he would pull out the little linen pouch that held their spoons.

But that moment never came. Private Chandler simply grunted. "Nothing here!" He replaced the mattress. Shocked, Rebecca glanced over at her sister, who looked as confused as she herself felt.

Private Chandler led the way down the ladder to the main room, with Priscilla and Ezekiel following him. Rebecca yearned to stay in the loft and search for the spoons, but she and Selinda had to remain with the others. They climbed down the ladder.

They were all in the main room when Widow Tyler walked in. She was carrying sacks of beans and cornmeal and she looked tired. When she saw Private Chandler, Priscilla, and Ezekiel assembled in her house, her eyebrows rose. "What's this about?"

Private Chandler explained that Ezekiel was searching for a knife that had been stolen from his cabin. "He says that Isaac took it, ma'am, but I didn't find it here."

"Of course not!" exclaimed the widow. She drew herself up. "How dare you search my house!"

"I know that savage took my knife," Ezekiel argued. "It must be here—"

"Hush!" the widow ordered. "Stealing is a serious offense, but so is falsely accusing someone! You could be punished for it." She glared at Priscilla. "Both of you!"

Priscilla's pretty face turned bright red. "Come, Ezekiel!" she ordered her brother, and without another word, she flounced from the house, with Ezekiel close behind her.

"Sorry to have upset your household, ma'am," Private Chandler said apologetically as he left. "Ezekiel seemed awful sure."

"Well, he was wrong," the widow announced firmly, and she closed the door behind the private. She turned and said something in Abenaki to Isaac. He nodded, then went back to his bed and closed the curtains.

The widow sank into her chair. "Imagine those Cutters searching here as if we're a bunch of common thieves!" she said, outraged. "That family thinks they are above everyone else in this fort!"

"Yes, ma'am," Rebecca agreed, but her mind was whirling. *What could have happened to the spoons?*

The widow turned to Selinda, and her voice softened. "I saw Mrs. Cutter while I was out. I tried to explain to her that you belong *here,* not in Connecticut. But that proud, stiff-necked woman as much as told me to mind my own affairs. I might as well have talked to a post."

The widow coughed violently, then she sighed. "I'm sorry, my dear," she told Selinda gently. "Perhaps when Captain Stevens returns, he can speak to Mrs. Cutter again. I hope he has more luck than I did."

"Thank you for trying, ma'am," Selinda said quietly. "May I make you a cup of tea?"

"No, I'm a bit tired," the widow said. She coughed again, then leaned back in her chair. "I think I'll rest."

In a few minutes, the widow was snoring gently. Rebecca motioned to Selinda to follow her up the ladder. As soon as they were in the loft, Rebecca pulled up the mattress. They both searched carefully underneath it, then checked the floor, the bedcover, their trunk— everywhere in the small, bare loft. Finally, they had to admit the truth: the spoons were gone. Even the small linen pouch was missing.

Panic rising, Rebecca turned to her sister. "Did you move the spoons anywhere?"

"No!" said Selinda, shocked at the suggestion. "I never would have moved them!"

Rebecca slumped on the bed. "Someone's taken them," she said, her voice as hollow as she felt inside. With the spoons gone, so was her hope of buying Selinda's freedom.

CHAPTER 7

SHADOWS AT NIGHT

For a moment, Rebecca and Selinda sat together in silence, trying to accept the terrible truth. Then Rebecca slammed her fist into her palm.

"It must be Isaac!" She spoke in a low tone so that only Selinda could hear her. "Old Johnny told me never to trust that white Indian boy, and he was right. Isaac must've snuck up here sometime yesterday when I was gone, and poked around till he found them."

Selinda shot her sister a troubled look. "But how could Isaac have known about the spoons?"

Rebecca thought for a moment. Then she realized what must have happened. "Do you recall the first night Isaac was here? We asked Captain Stevens whether we should sell the spoons. We thought Isaac couldn't understand, but I'll wager he knew every word."

Rebecca stood up. "I'll go get Private Chandler. That savage boy *is* a thief!"

Selinda grabbed her sister's arm. "Wait! We must be sure before we accuse him. Perhaps someone else knew the spoons were here—could that be?"

Rebecca paused. She considered Selinda's question. "Captain Stevens knew of the spoons, but he's away. Besides, he'd never steal anything," she said slowly. "I told Old Johnny about the spoons, but I never had a chance to show them to him."

"Old Johnny couldn't be a thief," Selinda said. "He's been trading at the fort for years. I remember him trading with Mama."

"That's so," Rebecca agreed. A shadow crossed her face as she recalled a sudden image of Mama standing in the sunlight of their farmyard, bargaining with Old Johnny. What had Mama been buying? Buttons? Cloth? A new pot? She couldn't remember now, but Selinda must be right. Old Johnny couldn't be the thief.

Rebecca searched her mind. Did anyone else know about the silver spoons? Suddenly, she remembered Ezekiel's sneering face. "Maybe Ezekiel."

"Ezekiel?" Selinda echoed.

"'Tis possible. Ezekiel heard me mention the spoons to Old Johnny," Rebecca recalled. "Then yesterday, I saw Ezekiel walking out our door. He said he'd been here looking for Isaac. But the widow was asleep, so who knows what he was really doing? He might've found the spoons and taken 'em."

Selinda looked shocked. "'Twould be a sin to do such a thing!"

Rebecca nodded. "'Twould be a sin, but Ezekiel might have thought he was very clever to have been able to find our spoons and then steal them." Rebecca paused. She was not sure that Ezekiel *was* that clever.

"Then again," she continued, "perhaps Ezekiel is right, and Isaac is the thief. After all, Isaac was raised by Indians, and Captain Stevens told me that he's used to taking whatever he wants."

"But Captain Stevens also told us to be kind to Isaac," Selinda reminded her gently. "We can't accuse him of being a thief if we're not sure."

"Aye," Rebecca said thoughtfully. She sat back down on the bed. She had a horrible, hollow feeling in her stomach, as if she had fasted too long. Mama had told her to keep the spoons, but now, when she needed them most, they had disappeared! Selinda looked at her anxiously.

"What should we do, Becca?"

Rebecca thought for a few moments. "We won't say a word to anyone now," she decided. "Captain Stevens should be back in two days. When he returns, we'll tell him everything. He'll know what to do. In the meantime—"

"Selinda!" Ezekiel's loud voice called from the Yard. "Mother says you're to come back to our house. Now."

"I must go," said Selinda reluctantly. "Mrs. Cutter will be angry if I'm away any longer."

"Very well," said Rebecca. "Keep an eye on Ezekiel. If he's the thief, maybe you can find out where he's put our spoons. I'll watch Isaac like a hawk. He may have a hiding place that Private Chandler didn't find." An idea occurred to her. "Perhaps that's where he went last night, when he was gone for so long."

"Selinda!" Ezekiel yelled. "You're going to be in trouble!"

"She's coming!" Rebecca shouted out to him, and Selinda started down the ladder.

From the loft's narrow window, Rebecca watched her sister limp across the Yard behind Ezekiel. They entered the Cutters' house, then Ezekiel closed the door behind them. It was hot in the loft, but Rebecca felt a cold rush of fear. *We must get the spoons back soon,* she realized, *or Selinda could be taken away forever.*

Selinda returned home late that evening. The Cutters had kept her hard at work until past sundown. Her narrow shoulders drooped with fatigue and her face looked drawn. Rebecca's heart ached for her sister, but they could not talk together freely until they had climbed to the loft for the night.

Once the girls were alone, Rebecca told her sister how she had carefully watched Isaac throughout the afternoon and evening.

"All he did was sleep, eat, whittle, and chop logs," Rebecca reported. "The only time he left the house, he was out at the woodpile."

"I *tried* to watch Ezekiel," Selinda said. "But Mrs. Cutter kept me busy 'most all the time. Still, when I saw him he seemed much as usual."

"Oh," said Rebecca, disappointed. For a moment, she was silent. Then she asked, "Selinda, if you had something to hide—something small—where would you put it?"

Selinda looked around the bare loft. "Here, I s'pose, but we already looked everywhere here."

"Yes, but what about Ezekiel's house? Tomorrow, when the Cutters are out, search through Ezekiel's things. Maybe he's hidden the spoons in his house."

"I'd feel like a thief!" Selinda protested.

"You won't be taking anything—you'll just be looking," Rebecca insisted. "As for me, first thing tomorrow, I'll look in the woodpile while Isaac's asleep. Maybe our spoons are hidden out there."

Selinda turned frightened eyes toward her sister. "We *will* find the spoons, won't we, Becca?"

"'Course we shall!" Rebecca replied confidently, but she wished she felt as sure as she sounded. She decided she would stay up all night and watch to see whether Isaac went out to the woodpile—or anywhere else in the fort. She did not tell Selinda about her plan. *There's no point in worrying her,* Rebecca told herself.

She lay in bed until she was sure Selinda was asleep. Then she quietly pulled her dress off its nail and slipped into it. If she heard Isaac leave, she wanted to be able to follow him as quickly as possible.

Once she was dressed, Rebecca sat on the edge of the bed and tried her best to stay awake. She bit her lip, counted backward, and even pinched herself. But the loft was warm, she'd had a tiring day, and the cabin was quiet. She couldn't help closing her eyes . . .

Suddenly Rebecca was awake. She realized that she'd been curled up on the bed. She wondered how long she'd been asleep.

She heard a door softly squeak on its hinges. *He's leaving!* Rebecca thought. She waited until the cabin was silent, then climbed down the ladder. She checked the door and window that led to the back. Both were barred from the inside; Isaac had not left that way. But the front door was slightly ajar. Rebecca opened the door carefully and stepped out into the Yard.

A breeze blew and the air had the damp smell of night. Rebecca shivered slightly as she stood by the widow's door and looked for signs of movement in the fort. She pressed her back against the rough wall and watched carefully. All she saw was a black cat stalking soundlessly across the hard-packed dirt. Everything seemed so different at night—the cabins cast eerie shadows in the moonlight, and the high palisade looked dark and menacing.

What if I find Isaac? Rebecca wondered. *What will happen then?* She recalled how fiercely the savage boy had fought with Ezekiel, and her mouth went dry with fear. For a moment, she wished she could go back inside the widow's cabin—back to where it was safe. Then she recalled how little time she and Selinda had before the Cutters left. *I can't go back now,* Rebecca resolved. *If Isaac's the thief, I must catch him.*

She took a deep breath. Then, gathering up the skirt of her faded homespun dress, she began to explore the fort's dark Yard. Cautiously, she hurried from one doorway to the next. Outside one house, she heard a small child calling "Mama!" At another, she heard someone snoring. There was no sign of Isaac anywhere. She had almost reached the South Gate when she decided to turn back; she could not risk the guards seeing her and questioning why she was outside in the middle of the night.

She retraced her steps toward Widow Tyler's cabin, thinking hard. The widow's back door and window had been barred from the inside, so Isaac must have left by the front door, which opened into the Yard. To leave the Yard, he would either have to enter a family's cabin or walk out the South Gate. Rebecca could not imagine him being foolish enough to barge into another family's house in the middle of the night. Nor could she imagine that the guards at the gate would allow him to leave the fort. *Isaac must be inside the Yard somewhere. But where?*

Rebecca was just a short distance from Widow Tyler's cabin when she saw a shadowy figure walking toward her. She hid in the darkness of a doorway. Then she realized it was a guard, patrolling the fort. He slowed in front of Widow Tyler's house.

Maybe the guard also suspects Isaac, Rebecca thought.

The guard tested the widow's front door and found it was not latched. As Rebecca peered from the shadows, she was shocked to see the guard open the door, then glance around, as if to check whether anyone observed him. He was about to step inside when he caught sight of Rebecca.

"Who goes there?" he called out nervously.

Rebecca recognized the voice. It was Ezekiel! She stepped out of the shadows. "What are you doing?" she demanded.

"Private Chandler said that since I'm almost sixteen, I can help patrol the fort," Ezekiel said defensively. "Your door was not latched." He paused, then asked suspiciously, "Why are you out here?"

"I was hot upstairs. I came out to get fresh air," Rebecca said as she brushed past Ezekiel and entered the widow's cabin. "Good night." She shut the door and quickly fastened the latchstring.

Her heart was pounding fast. She wondered what Ezekiel had really been doing—had he been trying to sneak inside? As she stood in the dark room, Rebecca heard the widow cough in her sleep. Then she heard the rustling

of bedcovers behind the curtains that hid Isaac's bed.
It sounded as if the boy were turning over in his sleep.

He's here! she realized. *How could he have come back
without me seeing him?*

Thoughts whirled in her mind as she climbed back
up to the loft. She hadn't checked Isaac's corner before
she left the house. Had he been in bed all along? Could
it have been Ezekiel—or someone else—that she'd heard
open the door earlier? Was Ezekiel truly on patrol? Or
was he trying to sneak into the widow's cabin?

Before Rebecca fell asleep, another thought struck
her. Maybe it *had* been Isaac who had opened the door—
but he hadn't been leaving the cabin, he'd been coming
back inside. If so, where had he been? And why?

Friday dawned as a perfect summer day, sunny and
clear. The air smelled of sweet summer grasses, and even
the birds seemed to sing more merrily than usual. It was
the kind of day that seemed to promise joy.

After the girls finished their morning chores, Selinda
left for the Cutters. The widow felt tired, so she stayed in
bed. Rebecca brought her breakfast: cornmeal mush and
a cup of steaming-hot tea mixed with honey. The widow
barely touched the mush, but she drank her tea gratefully.
Then she slipped back to sleep.

Isaac, too, stayed in bed. *This is my chance,* Rebecca thought. She unbarred the back door and stepped outside to the grassy area behind the house. The widow's woodpile had grown tremendously since Isaac's arrival, but as Rebecca looked at it, she shook her head with disapproval. The neighbors had neat, ordered piles with the logs stacked in tidy rows. Isaac's logs were thrown in a sprawling heap.

Rebecca decided to restack the wood—and search through the woodpile in the process. One by one, she picked up each log that Isaac had split, checked under it, then put it into a new pile. Creating neat stacks was harder work than she'd expected. Logs kept slipping or refusing to fit in rows. Soon her apron was covered with splinters and bark, and her face was damp with sweat.

Yet she was determined. By the time the sun had fully risen, Rebecca had built one woodpile as high as her chest and started on her second pile. A raven perched on top of the first stack of wood. It watched her intently.

Suddenly she heard an oddly accented voice ask, "Why?" She turned around. Isaac was standing behind her, pointing at the tidy log piles.

"'Tis better this way," Rebecca said, speaking slowly and clearly as if she were talking to a not-very-bright child. She gestured at the neighbors' neat woodpiles. "Like theirs."

"Why?"

Rebecca was flustered. "Well, it looks better," she said.

"And the logs will dry better too, I think." She returned to stacking the wood. "Anyway, this is the right way to do it. You should learn to do it this way."

For several minutes, Isaac continued to watch her. Finally he said, "English are like beavers." He pointed to the woodpile, then to the logs of the palisade, then to the log houses.

"Why, yes, I s'pose we are," Rebecca agreed, pleased that Isaac had finally begun to understand. "We work hard. We build homes for ourselves."

"Real beavers—good," Isaac said with a shrug. Then he gestured to the fort. "These beavers—no good."

"Huh!" Rebecca replied. "We've made a home out of this wilderness. Before we came here, this land was nothing."

Isaac stared at her hard. "Before you came, this was Indians' home."

Rebecca's cheeks flushed as if she'd been slapped. "You speak English," she accused him. "Why do you pretend you don't?"

For a moment, Isaac was silent. "Some people in my tribe talked English," he said finally. "They said I should not forget it. But I do not want to talk to English. Their soldiers are cowards. They shot my father in the back."

Rebecca was confused. "I thought your family was taken by Indians years ago."

"I have no memory of my white father. I speak of my

Indian father," Isaac corrected her. "That is my true family."

"But you were born white," Rebecca argued. "You'll always be white. Look." She held out her arm next to Isaac's. Even though he was more deeply tanned, she had naturally darker skin. Their arms were about the same color. "How can you say that the Indians are your true family?"

Isaac drew back his arm. Just then, the raven flew off into the sky, soaring high above the palisade. Isaac pointed at the bird. "Look," he said. "That bird was born in egg, but now he flies." He looked at Rebecca, his eyes slits of anger. "I was born white, but I am Abenaki now."

He turned and walked back to the cabin.

Rebecca watched him and wondered whether she should tell others in the fort that the savage boy really could speak English. But then she decided no. She was sure that Isaac would speak only when he wanted to. Besides, there would be time enough to tell everything when Captain Stevens returned. There was no point in stirring up more trouble now—at least not until the spoons were found.

She wiped her sweaty forehead and looked at her work. Suddenly, it seemed a little foolish to be spending so much time building a tidy pile of wood. She stacked the rest of the wood as quickly as possible, taking care to look under each log as she worked.

A speck of red caught her eye. She tugged at it and discovered a long red thread that had been caught on a piece of wood. She ran the thread between her fingers. It felt smooth and soft—not cotton, not linen. Silk, perhaps? But who in the fort would have a gown made of red silk? Not even Priscilla Cutter would wear such a fine dress.

Puzzled, Rebecca pocketed the thread and kept on working. She carefully examined each remaining log, but she saw nothing else unusual.

At noon Selinda came home for the midday meal. She looked pale, and she barely ate a bite of food. After the meal, when the two girls were alone, Selinda whispered to her sister that she had bad news: another family, the Polks, were leaving the fort on Monday. They were moving to safer land in the south, just as the Cutters were. The Cutters had decided to leave early so that they could travel with the Polks and a group of soldiers who would also be leaving that day.

"Mrs. Cutter says we must be ready to leave at the break of dawn on Monday," Selinda concluded. "Oh, Becca, what will I do?"

For a moment, the girls were silent. They were both thinking that today was Friday. There were only two more full days till Selinda had to leave—and one of those days was the Sabbath, when most of their waking hours would be spent in church.

"We must find the spoons!" said Rebecca. "Did you search Ezekiel's things?"

Selinda nodded. "The Cutters were out of the cabin quite a while, talking to the Polks. I looked as hard as I could, but I found nothing."

"Well, I found something in the woodpile." Rebecca pulled the red thread from her pocket. "What do you think of this?"

Selinda fingered the thread. Then she turned even paler.

"What?" Rebecca demanded. "Do you know what it's from?"

Selinda nodded. "I think so. It looks like a thread from Priscilla's red silk hair ribbon. 'Tis one of her favorites."

"What would a hair ribbon be doing in our woodpile?"

Selinda looked up at her sister. Her dark eyes were clouded with worry. "Priscilla was looking for her hair ribbon today. It had been drying by the window, but then it was gone. She said it'd been stolen."

CHAPTER 8

STOLEN!

"Isaac *must* be the thief," Rebecca declared. "He's the only one other than you and me who goes to our woodpile."

"I'm sorry to think of him as a thief—he was kind to me," Selinda said. She hesitated. "But if you're sure, should we tell Private Chandler?"

"I wish we could have Isaac arrested this very moment," Rebecca said bitterly. "But if he's in jail, he'll never lead us to the spoons. Besides, we still have no real proof." She held up the thread. "All we have is this."

"What should we do?"

Rebecca thought for a moment. "Captain Stevens should be home soon. We'll talk with him and tell him everything. He'll know what's best." She swallowed hard. "In the meantime, I'll sell some of our other things. We may need the money, just in case."

"Very well," Selinda agreed. She looked at her sister trustingly. "You know best."

I hope so, Rebecca thought. *I truly hope so.*

After Selinda left, Rebecca cleaned the dishes and made sure the widow was comfortable. Then she went up to the loft and carefully wrapped the heavy box of nails in Selinda's quilt. Her heart was beating fast and her hands felt clammy. She hated selling her family's things; she hated feeling like a beggar. She put on her only pair of shoes, even though they were too tight, and combed her hair neatly. *At least I can look respectable,* she thought. *Not as if I'm begging for charity.*

With her bundle in hand, Rebecca went outside to look for Old Johnny. She asked a few people if they'd seen the peddler. One man directed her to the blacksmith's shop, which was just outside the palisade.

When Rebecca came to the South Gate, the guard on duty warned her to go no farther than the blacksmith's shop, then let her pass. At the door to the shop, Rebecca stopped, wishing she did not have to go in. The blacksmith caught sight of her. "What do you want?" he called out gruffly.

Rebecca took a deep breath and stepped inside. The shop was dark and hot and smelled of smoking metal. The blacksmith was a bear of a man with arms as tough as the iron he hammered every day. "Excuse me, sir," said Rebecca. "Is Old Johnny here?"

There was a sizzling sound and a puff of smoke as the big man lifted a piece of metal up with his tongs

and set it down to cool in a bucket of water. Only after
the metal was cooled did he look up at Rebecca. "I s'pose
you could say he is." The blacksmith jerked his head
toward the back of the shop. "Johnny!" he called out.
"You've a visitor."

As Rebecca's eyes adjusted to the darkness, she saw
a crumpled heap in the corner of the shop. The heap
slowly unfolded and sat up. It was Old Johnny. His clothes
were dirty and he reeked of rum. He rubbed his bearded
chin. "Eh? What do you want?"

"I have some things to sell," said Rebecca.

Johnny squinted at her, as if he were trying to remember who she was. "I'm Rebecca Percy," she reminded him.
"I talked with you about my spoons."

"Spoons?" said Johnny. His eyes sharpened. "What
about the spoons?"

"I don't have them today," Rebecca said regretfully.
"But I have some other things to sell." She opened up
the quilt and pulled out the box of nails. "These nails are
very strong, and—"

"My head hurts," Johnny interrupted. He groaned
and sank back into the straw. "I'll talk to you another
time."

"Please, sir," Rebecca pleaded. "It's important that
I talk to you now."

"Go away!" the peddler ordered and turned his back
to her.

Rebecca slowly put the box away. "Hold on," said the blacksmith sternly. "Let me see those nails."

Surprised, Rebecca handed him the box, and he looked the nails over carefully. "Six shillings," he said at last.

Rebecca remembered how Papa had always bargained when he sold his crops. "Ten shillings," she told the blacksmith. "Those are very good nails."

He scowled at her. "Nine."

"Nine and a half," Rebecca countered.

The blacksmith stared from underneath his heavy brows. "Nine's my best offer."

Rebecca drew a deep breath. "Very well," she said. "Nine."

She gave the blacksmith the nails, then carefully placed the nine shillings in her drawstring purse. *Now we have twelve shillings in all,* she thought. *We still need twenty-eight more.*

She carried the quilt back to the fort and knocked at the Randolphs' cabin. Hannah opened the door. "Good day, Rebecca," she said cheerfully.

"Good day, I've—I've come to see your mother," Rebecca said, standing shyly on the threshold.

Mrs. Randolph came out from the back of the cabin. She held her youngest baby on her hip, and her four-year-old daughter, Mary, was pulling at her skirts. She had a welcoming smile on her face. For a moment, Rebecca felt a tug at her heart. She remembered how her mother used to carry Benjamin just the same way, and how she would smile at Rebecca when she came in from chores.

"Aye, what is it, Rebecca?" Mrs. Randolph asked. "Come in."

Rebecca walked inside. The cabin smelled deliciously of molasses, cinnamon, and freshly ground flour. "I wondered if perchance you'd be interested in buying this quilt, ma'am," Rebecca said. "Selinda made it."

Mrs. Randolph handed the baby to Hannah. Then she fingered the quilt. "Why are you selling it?"

Rebecca explained that she was raising money to buy back Selinda's contract from the Cutters. She decided not to tell Mrs. Randolph exactly how much money they owed on the contract—or how much they had already earned. *If I tell her we've so little,* she thought, *it'll seem I'm asking for charity.*

Mrs. Randolph listened to Rebecca carefully, then asked, "Have you thought that your sister might be better off with the Cutters? I know you'd miss her, but she *would* be safer in Connecticut, and I suppose . . ." Mrs. Randolph hesitated. "I *suppose* the Cutters would treat her decently enough."

"Selinda and I belong together," said Rebecca firmly. "We're family, all the family we have left right now. If she went away as far as Connecticut, we might never see each other again."

Mrs. Randolph looked at her, then glanced at Hannah,

who was holding the baby, and Mary, who stood close to her mother's side. "I suppose my children would feel the same way about each other if, heaven forbid, something should happen to their father and me." She sighed. "Let me look at this quilt."

She was examining the stitching when another knock came at the door. It was Mrs. Martin, a plump farmer's wife who had recently moved into the fort with her family. "Folks aren't safe anywhere these days!" Mrs. Martin announced as she marched in carrying her market basket.

Mrs. Randolph looked up, surprised. "What do you mean?"

Mrs. Martin took an empty flour sack out of her basket. "This is what I mean. Do you recall I bought flour yesterday?"

Mrs. Randolph nodded.

"I spent the whole day baking bread—seven loaves, big ones, too. We ate one loaf last night, and I left the rest out to cool on the window, thinking there were honest folks living here. Well, when I looked this morning, there were only three loaves left. Somebody stole three loaves of my bread! One of my cheeses is gone, too."

"Oh, no!" Mrs. Randolph exclaimed. "Are you sure it was a thief? Maybe a dog ate 'em."

"No dog could've ever jumped as high as that window," Mrs. Martin said. She looked around the store, as if to check for eavesdroppers, then added, "That's not the only theft I've heard of. One of the soldiers said someone took his jacket and a flint box. And the Walters say one of their blankets is missing." She looked hard at the quilt. "You didn't find that somewhere, did you?"

Rebecca said hurriedly, "My sister made that quilt—every stitch." She turned the quilt over and showed the neat, perfect lines of Selinda's sewing. "See?"

"Hmmm," said Mrs. Martin, eyeing Rebecca. "I heard Private Chandler was at your house, talking to that white Indian boy about a knife he stole from Ezekiel Cutter. If I don't miss my bet, that savage boy is at the root of all this."

Rebecca could not risk Isaac being arrested yet—she had to find the spoons first. She was sure that if Isaac were in jail, he would never tell where his hiding place was. "Private Chandler searched our house and Ezekiel's knife wasn't anywhere," she told Mrs. Martin. "For all we know, Ezekiel could have just lost it."

"And I suppose my breads sprouted legs and walked away—and took the cheese with them," Mrs. Martin replied sarcastically. She reached back into her basket. "In any event, I need more flour. I have some lovely fresh eggs to trade for it."

Mrs. Randolph measured out the flour, and Mrs. Martin counted out eggs in exchange. As Mrs. Martin was leaving, she fixed a stern gaze on Rebecca. "You'd better keep an eye on that white Indian boy," she warned. "If he's stealing things today, who knows what he'll try tomorrow."

"Yes, ma'am," Rebecca replied. *I shall watch him* very *carefully,* she told herself.

Mrs. Randolph returned to the quilt. After a few long moments, she looked up at Rebecca. "I don't usually buy quilts, but this one looks warm. I can give you four shillings for it."

Rebecca was disappointed, but she decided not to bargain with Mrs. Randolph. "Thank you, ma'am," she said, and put the four shillings in her drawstring purse.

She turned to leave, and Hannah called out to her, "Don't forget about the Johnsons' party!"

"Aye," said Rebecca absentmindedly. She had far more important things on her mind than a party. *How shall I get twenty-four more shillings? I must find the spoons!*

CHAPTER 9

A TERRIBLE FATE

When Rebecca returned home she found the widow in bed, coughing hard. Beside her was Isaac, sitting cross-legged on the floor. As soon as Rebecca came in, he stood up. Without a word, he retreated to his corner and closed the curtains.

Rebecca hurried to the widow's side. "I'm fine, dear," the widow assured her. "Ethan has been taking good care of me."

"Ethan?" Rebecca echoed.

The widow frowned slightly. "I meant to say Isaac. He's—" She was overcome by a fit of coughing. When it had passed, she finished her sentence. "He's a good boy. He made me tea."

Rebecca reached down and picked up the cup at the widow's side. She was surprised to find it was half full of hot tea sweetened with honey. *Why does he do kind things sometimes?* she wondered. *Is it so we won't suspect he's a thief?*

She busied herself fixing soup for their supper. Selinda came home, looking worn out from her long day at the Cutters. The two girls walked to the well so that they could talk in private.

"I sold the nails and the quilt," Rebecca whispered.

A shadow passed over Selinda's face, but she said nothing.

Rebecca read her sister's thoughts. "Papa will buy new nails to build us another house someday," she assured her. Then she patted her drawstring purse. "And now we've sixteen shillings. When we sell the spoons, we'll surely have enough to buy your contract."

Selinda brightened. "Do you know where the spoons are?" she asked eagerly.

"Nay," said Rebecca. "But I know Isaac's been taking other things, too."

Rebecca recounted the stories she had heard at the Randolphs'. Selinda nodded. "Aye, Ezekiel was talking about the thefts today. He says it's all Isaac's doing."

"Where can Isaac be hiding the things?" Rebecca wondered aloud. "He might have eaten the bread and cheese—I think he'd eat a whole moose if we gave it to him—but he didn't eat a blanket or a jacket. Where could they be?"

In low tones, the sisters discussed the possibilities. Could Isaac have found a secret hiding place inside the small, crowded fort? Or could he be leaving the fort at night—and hiding the things somewhere in the woods?

"How could he escape the fort and then return, all without the guards seeing him?" Selinda questioned. "And why would he steal a blanket and food? It's not cold, and we give him plenty to eat."

"Mayhap he plans to run away," Rebecca suggested. She glanced out through the palisade at the wooded hills that loomed in the distance, beyond the fort. "But he wouldn't have much chance traveling in the forest alone."

"'Twould be a hard journey to Canada, wouldn't it?" Selinda asked.

Rebecca nodded. As they walked back to the widow's cabin, both girls thought about their parents and Ben and what it must have been like for them to travel that long way with the Indians. "I don't know where Isaac's hiding place is," Rebecca said finally. "But I mean to find out. I wish we could search his things again. It seems he's always about the cabin."

Soon after the sisters arrived home, Hannah Randolph knocked at the door. She was wearing her best dress, and she looked at the girls' aprons in surprise. "Are you not coming to the party?" Hannah asked. "We shall be leaving soon."

"Oh, I'm sorry," Rebecca stammered. In her worries about Isaac and the spoons, she'd forgotten all about the Johnsons' party. "I'm afraid I won't be able to go. I must stay here."

The widow looked up. She'd awakened from her nap feeling better, and she was now sitting in her chair with her Bible. "You girls may go, if you wish. A party would do you good. Isaac could go with you."

"Oh no, ma'am," Selinda said quickly. "I'm too tired to go all that way."

"What about you, Isaac?" the widow asked. She said something to him in Abenaki. Isaac thought for a moment, then he stood up, as if ready to leave.

"That's settled then," the widow said, pleased. "You and Isaac go to the party, Rebecca. Selinda and I shall stay here."

Rebecca stood in the center of the cabin, frozen with indecision. Out in the Yard, she heard noise and laughter as several families prepared to leave for the Johnsons' farm.

"Go," Selinda urged. "We'll be fine here."

Suddenly, Rebecca smiled. "Very well, we'll go." She took off her apron and handed it to her sister. As she did so, she made sure her back was to Isaac and Hannah. She whispered to Selinda, "Search Isaac's things while we're gone."

Selinda looked surprised, but she nodded ever so slightly.

Rebecca put on her too-tight shoes, and she, Hannah, and Isaac headed out to the Yard. The sun was beginning to set over the western palisade. In the Yard, the men

all carried muskets, and a few people held torches high.
When everyone was assembled, the guard opened the
South Gate.

"Have a merry time," the guard shouted after them.
"And drink some flip for me!"

It was less than a quarter mile to the Johnsons' farm,
and the crowd walked quickly, full of anticipation for
the evening that lay ahead. Hannah chatted excitedly
to Rebecca. "I wonder who will dance with me tonight—
'tis so long since I've danced!" she said.

She whispered to Rebecca the names of all the boys
she would like to dance with—and all the boys she
wouldn't dream of dancing with. Both girls were glad
the Cutters were not coming to the party. "I'd *never*
want to dance with Ezekiel," Hannah said, making a
face. Rebecca nodded in agreement.

Then Hannah pointed at Isaac. "And can you imagine
dancing with a savage boy like that?" she said loudly
enough for Isaac to hear. She giggled. "Bet all he knows
is Indian dances!"

Rebecca was sure Isaac understood some, if not all,
of Hannah's comment. His face, however, was as blank
as ever. He walked quietly at the edge of the crowd,
watching everything but saying nothing.

As they neared the Johnsons' farm, Rebecca heard
the sweet, lilting sound of fiddles drifting out the open
window. Six-year-old Sylvanus Johnson stood at the door

to meet the partygoers. "Welcome, welcome!" he called out, lisping through his missing front teeth. "The party is starting!"

The Johnsons' party was a lively affair. Even though Mrs. Johnson was about to give birth to her fourth child, she worked hard to put out plenty of food, and Miriam poured cup after cup of punch for the guests. Dancers filled the cabin and spilled out into the farmyard.

Rebecca tried to enjoy herself, but she could not put the mystery of Isaac and the spoons out of her head. Every time she looked up, she saw Isaac standing silently in the shadows. Some of the settlers joked about the white Indian boy, while others shot him hostile glances.

"He doesn't belong here," Rebecca heard one man say. "I wonder why he came." Silently, Rebecca agreed with the man. *Isaac doesn't belong here,* she thought resentfully. Then a sudden question struck her: *I wonder where he does belong?*

Rebecca and Isaac joined the first group of guests— mostly families with young children—to leave the party. Their walk back to the fort was more tense than the happy stroll to the party had been. The night was now pitch-black, and the group was smaller. The men held their muskets ready and peered out into the darkness of the forest as they walked. Rebecca noticed that even Isaac seemed particularly alert—watching and listening with every step.

They reached the fort safely and found the widow
was asleep. Selinda was waiting up for them. "I have good
news," she announced with a smile. "While you were gone,
Captain Stevens and his men came back. I heard the sentry
welcoming them."

"He's back!" Rebecca exclaimed. She felt a wave of
relief. "Thank heavens!" She looked over toward Isaac,
but he had already disappeared into his curtained corner.

"Did you search Isaac's things?" Rebecca whispered
to her sister.

"Aye, as soon as the widow fell asleep, I went through
everything," Selinda replied. "I looked everywhere I could
think of, but I found nothing."

Rebecca tried to hide her disappointment. She knew
how careful her sister could be. If Selinda hadn't found the
spoons, they probably were not in the cabin. "First thing
in the morning, we'll go talk to the captain," Rebecca
whispered. "He'll know what to do."

After Selinda climbed the ladder to their loft, Rebecca
made sure the windows and the back door were barred,
and she pulled in the latchstring of the front door. By the
time she got into bed, Selinda was already asleep.

For a few moments, Rebecca lay in bed and listened
to the sounds outside. Another group of partygoers was
returning from the Johnsons' farm. They were laughing
and talking in the Yard. Rebecca found the noise soothing.
Isaac won't slip out tonight, she told herself. *There are too*

many people about. And tomorrow I'll talk to Captain Stevens. With that comforting thought, she drifted into a deep, peaceful sleep.

Soon after dawn, she was awakened by an explosion of noise.

The warning guns! Rebecca realized. Her stomach churned with fear. She threw on her homespun dress and rushed down the ladder, with Selinda following close behind. The widow, who could sleep through almost anything, was still snoring in her bed. Isaac was standing by the open window, looking out into the Yard.

Rebecca hurried past him. The settlers, some still in their nightclothes, were gathering in the Yard. She could hear voices raised in anger.

"We could leave now," Captain Stevens was saying. "We could probably catch them. This time we could teach them a lesson."

"No!" insisted Lieutenant Willard. "I can't risk the lives of my daughters and grandchildren. If the Indians see us in pursuit, they'll kill them all."

The sick feeling in Rebecca's stomach grew. She looked toward the northeast and saw plumes of smoke rising in the air. *The Johnsons' farm!* She heard the sound of crying behind her. She whirled around to see Mrs. Randolph and Hannah.

Rebecca was filled with dread. "What's happened?"

Sobbing, Mrs. Randolph explained that Aaron Hosmer, the Johnsons' hired man, had come running into the fort yelling that the Johnsons' farm had been attacked.

"They all went to bed late 'cause of the party," said Mrs. Randolph. "A dozen savages woke 'em up just before daybreak."

Rebecca heard a sharp intake of breath. It was Selinda. She had joined Rebecca, and now, listening to the tale, she looked paler then ever. She slipped her small, callused hand into her sister's. "Did any of the family escape?" she asked.

Mrs. Randolph shook her head. The Indians had captured Miriam Willard, Mr. and Mrs. Johnson and their three little children, and two hired men. Aaron Hosmer had escaped by hiding under a bed when the Indians searched the cabin. He had fled just before they set fire to the building.

"We were all so happy together last night," said Mrs. Randolph, wiping a tear from her eye. "I promised Susanna I'd help her when the baby came. And now to think it may be born in the wilderness without even a midwife! What a terrible fate!"

"And poor Miriam!" Hannah echoed. "What will she—"

The crack of a musket interrupted her. Lieutenant Willard was standing on a barrel in the center of the Yard. He'd fired the shot to get everyone's attention. Rebecca was shocked by the lieutenant's appearance. He looked as if he had aged ten years in a single morning. "For the safety of the captives, we have decided not to pursue the savages," he said in a deep, somber voice.

A murmur of sympathy spread through the crowd. Everyone knew how hard it must be for Lieutenant Willard to see his daughters, Susanna Johnson and Miriam Willard, and his beloved grandchildren taken captive. Yet it was well known among the colonists that the Indians would kill their captives rather than surrender them.

"We'll double our efforts to protect the fort. There may be more Indian raiding parties out there," Lieutenant Willard continued. As he said this, the gates opened, and Captain Stevens strode out to join the mounted soldiers waiting just outside the fort. Captain Stevens jumped onto his horse, and he and his men galloped away.

Captain Stevens is gone, Rebecca realized as she watched the gates close. She had a sinking feeling inside. *I never had a chance to ask him for his help!*

"Captain Stevens will patrol the area," the lieutenant said. "There'll be extra patrols and extra guards. Everyone should keep close to the fort. Our enemies could be any-where."

"What about an enemy *in* the fort?" called out some-one from the crowd. Rebecca recognized Ezekiel's voice. "What about the white Indian boy?"

"What about him?" the lieutenant asked sharply.

"He went to the Johnsons' party last night, didn't he?

Mayhap he slipped off and told the Indians all about it. He could have told 'em the Johnsons were easy pickings."

Again there was a murmur in the crowd, but this time it was not so friendly. "Maybe that savage boy did have something to do with the raid," a farmer told his neighbor.

"Wouldn't surprise me," the neighbor replied.

No. No, it can't be! Rebecca thought frantically.

Lieutenant Willard jumped off the barrel and strode to the South Gate. The settlers followed him, and Rebecca struggled to get to the front of the crowd. She felt the settlers' anger growing as hot as a bonfire. *What will happen?* she worried.

Lieutenant Willard turned to the sentry. "You were on guard last night," he said. "Did you see the white Indian boy go out of the fort?"

"Yes, sir," said the sentry. "He went with the others to the party, but he came back early, with the first group of folks."

"Did he go out again?"

"No, sir."

"Are you sure?"

"Yes, sir."

Lieutenant Willard looked around at the settlers who had gathered behind him. "If any of you have *proof* that the white Indian boy helped the Indians with last night's attack, I want to know about it. The punishment for treason is hanging, and I'd gladly hang anyone who betrayed my family."

The lieutenant paused, as if waiting for someone to speak up. Rebecca was silent, but she felt guilt like a pile of heavy stones on her shoulders. *Was it my fault that the Johnsons were attacked?* she wondered. *What if I had told the soldiers about Isaac's nighttime wandering? Would it have made a difference?*

Lieutenant Willard continued. "As far as I can tell, the boy was here all night, and I will not hang an innocent man—or boy." Suddenly, the lieutenant looked even more tired than before. He waved his hand at the crowd. "Go home, everyone. Look after your families. And don't leave the fort."

Slowly the settlers walked away. Mrs. Cutter demanded that Selinda come to her cabin. The two sisters exchanged a glance; then Rebecca nodded, signaling her sister that they would talk later. Selinda followed Mrs. Cutter, and Rebecca returned home alone to Widow Tyler's. As she entered the house, she saw that the widow was still sleeping. Isaac stood looking out the window. His face was expressionless, and his lack of emotion infuriated Rebecca.

"Look what your Indian friends have done," she said, pointing to the column of smoke rising from the Johnsons' farm. "They've destroyed an innocent family!"

Isaac glared at her. "Your soldiers have burned all of

an Indian village," he said coldly. Then he strode back to his corner, pulling the curtains shut behind him.

Suddenly, Rebecca felt as unsteady as a newborn calf. She sank to the bench beside the table. Her mind whirled with doubts. Should she have told Lieutenant Willard that Isaac sometimes wandered about the fort at night? Had she been wrong to keep it a secret?

Yet as far as she knew, Isaac had not gone out last night. She remembered the major's angry looks and his threat of hanging a traitor. She had a sudden vision of Isaac dangling from gallows in the center of the fort's Yard. And what if he was innocent? He might be a thief but not a traitor.

We must have more proof, Rebecca decided at last. *I'll wait and watch Isaac tonight—no matter what happens.*

CHAPTER 10

INTO THE WILDERNESS

As the sun rose on the fort that day, the air grew thick and hot. The sky looked as if it wanted to rain but was holding back. The settlers went about their chores out of habit, but their minds were on the tragic events of the morning.

They gathered in clumps and discussed the attack. Some people pointed a finger at Isaac, saying that the white Indian boy was trouble and had somehow had a hand in the raid. Others said the raid was a warning sign from God. Still other settlers saw the attack as the start of another war.

"We're in for trouble with those French and Indians," one soldier advised. "No one will be safe."

Selinda came home from the Cutters as if she were in a fog. "All day long, people came and talked about the raid," she told Rebecca. "'Twas almost more than I could bear. I kept remembering—" She broke off.

Rebecca held her sister's hand. "I know," she said.

That night, as soon as Selinda fell asleep, Rebecca climbed out of bed and put her dress back on. She sat upright on the hard wooden floor, willing herself to stay awake in case Isaac left the house. *I can't fail—I simply can't. I must find the spoons. And I must find out what Isaac is doing at night.*

It was a long night. Twice Selinda awoke screaming, gasping in terror from the horrors of her nightmares. Again and again, Rebecca comforted her. "I'm here. All is well."

"And Mama and Papa will come back? And Benjamin?"

"Of course they will," Rebecca said. "Mama promised they would."

"And no one will separate us?" Selinda asked.

"I won't let them," Rebecca assured her. *But how?* she wondered. *How?*

After each of the nightmares, it took Rebecca almost an hour to get her sister back to sleep. She was sure, however, that Isaac was at home during that time. She listened carefully to his breathing downstairs and heard him moving in his sleep.

In the middle of the night, there was a heavy knocking at the door. Rebecca hurried down the ladder and looked out. It was Ezekiel, carrying a lantern and his musket. "I'm on guard duty tonight," he announced as Rebecca unlatched the door. "I'm checking to be sure that white Indian boy is here."

He elbowed his way past Rebecca and shone his light into Isaac's corner. Isaac was lying on the bed asleep—or pretending to be. "Huh," Ezekiel grunted and stalked out the door.

Rebecca returned to the loft and struggled to stay awake until the sun sent a hazy light across the eastern horizon. Then, finally, she allowed herself to drift off to sleep. Her last thought was, *I'm sure Isaac did not leave the house in the night. Was he just being cautious—or have I been wrong about him after all?*

Sunday morning dawned cool and rainy, with a cloud of fog hanging over the river valley. The dismal weather matched Rebecca's spirits. She felt tired from her sleepless night and filled with anxiety.

It was the Sabbath, though, so she splashed cold water on her face and neatly combed her hair to prepare for Sunday worship. Selinda scrubbed her face and tied back her brown curls. They both put on their shoes and their best Sunday aprons. Then they were ready for church.

The widow talked to Isaac in Abenaki and somehow—Rebecca couldn't guess how—convinced him to go to church with them. They all walked together down the length of the fort's Yard. The widow leaned on Isaac's arm. Rebecca and Selinda followed behind.

"Today I will pray to God for a miracle," Selinda told her sister as they walked together arm in arm. "A miracle that will let me stay here with you."

We'll need a miracle, Rebecca thought. *Either that or the silver spoons.* She saw Ezekiel Cutter walking toward them. He was now dressed in his Sunday clothes, but there was still a sneer on his face. He stared at Isaac, then announced, "So now they are letting heathen savages into church!"

The widow raised her hand to one ear. "Eh?" she asked. "What's that?" Isaac acted as if he had not heard anything.

Ezekiel followed them as they filed into the building and walked upstairs to the Great Chamber, where the Sunday services were held. It was a large, open room filled with rows of narrow wooden benches. The chamber's windows overlooked the fields surrounding the fort. There were small, narrow windows, which were just large enough to aim a musket through. There were also bigger windows with heavy shutters that could be fastened from within in case of attack.

Widow Tyler found a bench near the back. Ezekiel took a seat right behind them. Whenever Rebecca glanced back, she saw Ezekiel staring at Isaac like a cat that had cornered a field mouse. Rebecca felt her tension growing as she waited for the church service to begin.

Finally, the elder who was leading the church service walked into the Great Chamber carrying his Bible. All

the settlers stood up. Isaac, with a little prodding from
the widow, rose to his feet, too. Then he crossed himself.
Rebecca heard an outcry from behind her.

"Look!" Ezekiel called out. "He made the sign that
the French do!" Everyone turned and saw Ezekiel pointing
at Isaac.

Ezekiel imitated how Isaac had gestured with his right
hand, making the sign of the cross against his body. There
was an angry murmur among the churchgoers, and one of
the pew minders stepped forward. It was Mr. Thompson,
a husky man who was responsible for maintaining order
in the church. He pulled Isaac off his bench. "We'll have
none of that here," he said roughly.

"The boy meant no harm. He was only doing what he's
been taught," the widow protested. "He must have learned
it from a French missionary."

"We'll learn him different," Mr. Thompson declared.
He pushed Isaac out the door, and Rebecca heard a heavy
clumping on the stairs. She saw Ezekiel grin. Other settlers looked relieved that the white Indian boy was
now gone. But Rebecca felt troubled. As much as she dis-
trusted Isaac, she did not believe that he had meant to do
wrong by crossing himself.

"Isaac doesn't know our ways yet," Selinda whispered.
"Why did they punish him?"

"I don't know," Rebecca replied, but she'd seen the
eyes of the people seated around her. She realized that

they hated Isaac because he was still too much like an Indian. For the first time, she wondered what would happen after Isaac's kin came from New York to fetch him. Would he ever be truly accepted?

The morning church service lasted four hours. For Rebecca, it seemed to drag on forever. Several times she nodded off to sleep, only to be awakened by a nudge from Selinda's elbow or a hard tap from Mr. Thompson's long stick.

Finally, the service was over. Rebecca and Selinda were walking home with Widow Tyler when Mrs. Cutter overtook them. "Selinda!" she called out in her shrill voice. "Remember—the soldiers are riding out at first light tomorrow morning. Our family and the Polks shall ride with them. See that you are packed and ready."

The widow frowned. "Amelia Cutter, this is the Sabbath! You can't expect the child to work at packing her things on the Sabbath."

Mrs. Cutter pointedly ignored the widow. "See that you are ready," she repeated to Selinda. "Anything you don't have prepared will be left behind. Good day!" Then she marched off.

"Some people think only of themselves!" the widow said angrily at Mrs. Cutter's back. Then she turned and put her arm around Selinda's narrow shoulders. "I am so sorry you must leave, my dear," she said, her voice cracking slightly. "I shall pray for you every day."

"Thank you, ma'am," Selinda said, her head hung low.

Rebecca did not trust herself to speak. Selinda's time was running out quickly, and she did not know how to save her. She was so angry that she found a stone and kicked it across the Yard.

She followed it with her eye and watched it land next to Old Johnny, who was walking in the opposite direction. He looked rumpled this morning but he seemed sober.

A desperate plan occurred to Rebecca. "Excuse me, ma'am," she told the widow. She quickly crossed the Yard. "Good day, sir!" she called to Old Johnny. "May I speak with you?"

He glanced up and a look of recognition crossed his face. "I don't do business on the Sabbath," he said, and tried to walk past her.

Rebecca flushed with embarrassment, but she continued. "I know, but I have some things I must sell by dawn tomorrow."

"I told you, child, I don't want to talk business."

"Please, sir!" Rebecca pleaded. "'Tis very important. I could meet you here in the Yard tomorrow—before first light."

The peddler looked around the Yard. A few settlers were watching them curiously. "Very well," he agreed at last. "I'll meet you here, at first light tomorrow."

"Thank you!" said Rebecca.

Rebecca returned to the widow's house with a glimmer

of hope in her heart. Now, if she could find the spoons, she would be able to sell them before the Cutters left. If she couldn't find the spoons, she would offer the peddler everything she and Selinda owned except the clothes on their backs. She would sell their last blanket, their winter clothes, and even their shawls. She wasn't at all sure what their few remaining belongings would earn, but it was the last hope she had—and she clung to it.

At home, Rebecca found the widow dozing in her chair, the Bible open in her lap. Isaac sat whittling with the long knife. Rebecca wondered what had happened to him after he had been thrown out of church, but as usual, Isaac was silent.

The widow did not allow the girls to work on the Sabbath, so they had a cold dinner. The rain was falling heavily now, and it was gloomy inside the cabin. Widow Tyler read aloud from the Bible and said prayers until the bell tolled for the late-afternoon church service. Rebecca and Selinda prepared to leave, but the widow said she was tired. "I'll stay here. Isaac can remain here as well."

Rebecca and Selinda stepped out into the muddy Yard. The rain had settled into a heavy, gray mist. "'Tis so foggy out here," said Selinda. "'Tis almost like evening."

"Aye," said Rebecca thoughtfully. "'Tis almost like evening." A sudden suspicion occurred to her. "Selinda, I'm going back to the house. If anyone asks where I am, tell them I'm home taking care of the widow."

Selinda's brow furrowed. "That would be the truth, wouldn't it?"

"Yes," Rebecca lied. "It would be true." She paused. "And Selinda, keep praying for a miracle."

Selinda smiled. "I shall."

Rebecca watched her sister limp into the fog, then she turned back as if she were headed home. But instead of returning to the widow's house, Rebecca stopped next door at the Grays' lean-to. The lean-to was a simple shack. It had walls on three sides, but the fourth side, which faced the Yard, was open. The Grays had a cabin outside the fort, but they stayed in their lean-to whenever there was threat of Indian attack. This afternoon, the family had gone to church, and the lean-to was deserted.

Rebecca stood in the shadows and waited. *God forgive me for lying to my sister,* she thought, *but I must know whether Isaac leaves the fort.*

Hidden in the shadows of the lean-to, Rebecca kept an eye on the widow's house. She watched and waited, looking first out the front of the lean-to, then checking the back window. She saw no one except the guards.

She was beginning to wonder if she had made a mistake, when she caught a movement behind the widow's cabin. A thin figure slipped out of the back window and, with movements as stealthy as a bobcat, disappeared into the mist.

He shan't get away this time, Rebecca vowed to herself.

She hitched up her petticoats and climbed out the Grays'
back window. She looked around for the thin figure. She
couldn't see him anywhere.

The stretch of land between the houses and the palisade seemed empty. The only sounds were the patter of
rain and occasional voices that filtered out from the worship service. Rebecca crept across the open space and hid
behind the woodpile.

Suddenly, she heard someone approaching. It was the
guard making his rounds. For a moment, Rebecca considered calling the guard and telling him that Isaac had run
away from the widow's house. But she still did not know
where the spoons were hidden. And she was sure that if
Isaac were arrested, he would never admit to stealing anything.

I must follow him myself, Rebecca decided. *Once I find
where he's hidden the spoons, then I'll alert the guards.*

As the guard came closer, Rebecca felt her heart
pounding. She flattened herself against the woodpile, her
nose pressed into the earthy smell of the wet logs. The
guard passed by, whistling softly to himself. Then everything was quiet again. Rebecca peered into the mist.
Where can Isaac be? she wondered. *Have I lost him already?*

Then she saw a shadowy movement by the palisade.
A figure swiftly emerged from the darkness and lifted
himself hand over hand up the fourteen-foot-high log.
He climbed so quickly and easily that Rebecca could

scarcely believe it. She remembered how Private Chandler
had declared that Isaac could climb faster than a squirrel.
So that's how he's been escaping the fort, thought Rebecca.
Within moments, Isaac was over the palisade and down
on the ground below. Briefly, he stood motionless against
the palisade, and then he headed down a path that led to
the river.

Rebecca felt her stomach knot with fear as she watched
Isaac disappear into the fog. There was danger beyond the
palisade—wild animals and, worse, savage Indians. Yet if
she were ever to discover what Isaac had been doing, she
had to follow him. Now.

She ran to the northwest corner of the palisade and
found the gap where she had once been able to enter the
fort. She took a deep breath and tried to wiggle through
the opening. At first, she thought she could no longer pass
between the logs. She had grown too much. Then she
exhaled, forcing all the air out of her chest. She pushed as
hard as she could. Suddenly she was out of the fort. She
hurried down the path Isaac had taken.

The path headed northwest, past her family's farm and
toward the river. When her family had lived together on
the farm, they had taken this route frequently. But never
before had Rebecca walked it alone or in a fog. The old
path, which once seemed so familiar, now looked strange.
Trees loomed in the darkness, and at every turn Rebecca
wondered whether there was an Indian waiting, poised to

attack her. She imagined the tomahawk, aimed straight for her head. *Would anyone hear me scream?*

As she headed farther and farther from the safety of the fort, Rebecca wished desperately that she could turn back. But she thought of Selinda and what would happen if they couldn't find the spoons. She kept on going. She walked as quietly as she could and listened to all the sounds around her. There were rustling leaves and steady rain. But she could not hear any footsteps.

The path came to a fork. One side led uphill to the north, past the old farm. The other side led downhill, west to the river. Rebecca hesitated and then heard a slight noise uphill, as if someone had stepped on a stick. She froze. Although the evening was cool and her dress was drenched with rain, she broke into a sweat. *Was it Isaac?*

After a few moments of silence, she carefully turned and made her way up the hill. At the top, the forest cleared. There was an open field, and Rebecca could see the ruins of her family's home outlined against the sky. She could see a figure outlined against the sky, too. It was Isaac.

She crouched by the edge of the woods, not far from Fairyland. She watched Isaac walk through the burned remains of her family's cabin. He opened the door to the old root cellar and climbed inside. After a few moments, he came up out of the cellar. Then he disappeared into the woods.

Rebecca waited and watched until, finally, curiosity overpowered her fear. She hurried across the open field and through the ruins of the cabin. She hesitated for a moment when she saw the cellar door. Unlike the building around it, it had not been damaged by the fire. The thick wooden door in the ground looked much as it had when the building was whole.

The trapdoor brought back a flood of painful memories. In her mind, she could see Mama leaning over the open trapdoor. "Watch over your sister," Mama had said. "I'm counting on you."

I must do this, Rebecca told herself. *I must.*

She gritted her teeth and pulled up the heavy cellar door. Then the smell wafted up to her—the same odor of old potatoes and damp earth that she remembered. She forced herself to climb down the wooden ladder. It creaked under her weight. At the base of the ladder, her foot pressed against something. She put her hand down and felt what seemed to be a blanket with items bundled up inside it.

Quickly, she grabbed the bundle and hurried out of the cellar, leaving the door open behind her. As soon as she was outside, she looked down at the bundle in her arms. It was tied together with Priscilla's red silk hair ribbon.

He is the thief! Rebecca thought.

She tore off the ribbon and opened the blanket.

Wrapped inside, she found a man's heavy jacket, three loaves of bread, a brick of cheese, and a flint box. But where were the spoons? Had she missed them somehow in the darkness? She looked through the sleeves of the jacket and felt inside the pocket. There was nothing. Could the spoons have dropped from the blanket when she opened it? She had just begun to search the ground when she felt sharp steel against her throat.

"What are you doing here?" a low voice demanded from behind her.

CHAPTER **11**

TRAPPED

It was Isaac. His arms pinned her from the back, and his knife pressed against her throat.

"I have a right to be here," Rebecca stammered. "'Tis my parents' farm. Let me go!"

"You would run to the fort. You would tell soldiers I am here," Isaac said. His voice was cold with anger.

For a moment Rebecca was silent. She knew it was her duty to tell the soldiers about Isaac. But she couldn't admit to that, not with a knife at her throat.

"I shan't tell anyone," Rebecca promised. "I haven't yet told that you've gone from the fort at night."

"You knew?"

She tried to nod, but Isaac held her too tightly. "Who else knows?" he demanded.

"Only Selinda, and she wouldn't tell. She liked you. I guess she was wrong."

Isaac released his grip on her. "Why did you not tell the soldiers?" he asked.

Rebecca stepped away, then turned and faced him. "At first I wasn't sure," she said, "and then . . ." She paused.

"What?"

"Then, I was afraid they'd hang you. As bad as you are, I didn't think you deserved to die."

Isaac stared at her hard for a few moments, as if he were deciding something. Then he tucked the knife back into his belt. Rebecca noticed its distinctive white handle. There were two letters carved on it: *E.C.*

"Go back to the fort," Isaac ordered her. "Say nothing to anyone. Soon, I will be gone."

"You're running away?"

"I'm going home," he said simply. "My father is dead. My family needs me." He crouched on the ground and began to retie his bundle. "I would have left before, but guards were watching. The rain tonight is good."

Rebecca pointed to the items on the ground. "You stole those things—didn't you?" she demanded. "And you took Ezekiel's knife."

A slight smile crossed Isaac's face. "I did not take the knife," he said. "He hid it in my bed. He wanted to trap me. I put it in the woodpile before he brought the soldier."

"I looked through the woodpile," Rebecca said. "There was nothing there."

"After the soldier searched, I found this place. It was

hidden, and animals could not get the food."

"But you're stealing!" Rebecca protested.

Isaac cinched the bundle tightly. "If a white man ran from the Indians, would he not take things he needed?"

Rebecca was confused. "That would be different!"

"Why?" Isaac demanded.

"Well . . ." Rebecca began. She couldn't quite explain why, but it had to be different. "It simply is," she said.

"English think nothing of tricking Indians or stealing from us," Isaac said. He stood up. "When my tribe adopts captives, we treat them as brothers. Not the way you treated me, like a savage animal."

He looked directly at Rebecca, but she said nothing.

"Some captives stay and become our true brothers," Isaac continued. "Others try to get free. One white boy pretended to be sick. His Indian mother believed him and took him to a white doctor. The doctor helped the boy run away. His mother did not eat for days. To her, the boy was not a captive. He was a son."

"But *you're* not a captive here," Rebecca argued. "You're white. You're one of us."

"I'll never be one of you. And I *am* captive here. Why else do your soldiers keep me inside? Why do you spy on me?"

Rebecca drew herself up to her full height. "I wasn't spying on you. I had to find out where you'd hidden our silver spoons."

"Silver spoons?" Isaac echoed. "You followed me here for spoons?"

Anger brought a flush to Rebecca's cheeks. "I need them to buy Selinda's freedom back from the Cutters!"

"You think I have these spoons?"

"I know you do," Rebecca said with more courage than she knew she had. She put out her hand. "Give them back to me," she demanded.

A smile flickered across Isaac's face. "You are not a coward. But you are wrong. I know nothing of your spoons."

"Don't lie. You must have them."

He shouldered his bundle. His face was serious again. "I have only what I need for my journey. I have no spoons."

Rebecca began to believe him. But she could not give up hope so easily.

"Those spoons are important to Selinda and me. Do you swear you didn't take them? Swear on . . ." She tried to think of something Isaac might value. "Swear on whatever's most holy to you."

"I swear," he said, looking her straight in the eye. "I swear on my family."

Rebecca stared into his face for a long moment. "Aye," she said at last. "I believe you."

She turned around, her shoulders slumped with disappointment. Suddenly, Isaac grabbed her arm. "Shhhh! Someone comes."

With one swift, strong movement, he pushed Rebecca

toward the open trapdoor. She almost fell, but she caught the ladder just in time and half stumbled, half dropped into the dark cellar.

Isaac snatched up his bundle and jumped into the cellar beside her. He landed almost soundlessly on the dirt floor. He placed his finger to his lips and motioned to Rebecca to be silent. Then he stepped onto the first rung of the ladder, reached up, and quietly pulled the heavy trapdoor closed over his head.

Rebecca felt a wave of panic as the last bit of light was shut out from the cellar. "No!" she protested, and tried to push Isaac aside. "No, don't!"

Isaac pressed his hand across her mouth and pinned down her arms. She struggled to get free, panic rising inside her like an animal clawing to get out.

Then she heard him whisper, "If you be quiet, I let you go."

She nodded, and Isaac dropped his hand and freed her arms. Rebecca took a great gulp of air. It was moist and cold.

Isaac leaned toward her. "Listen," he whispered, close to her ear. Rebecca listened hard and she could hear voices above. *Was it Indians?* she wondered. *Or soldiers from the fort?* At first, the voices were too far away for her to understand. Then they drew closer. They were Indians.

She felt sick to her stomach. *It can't be happening again,* she thought. But it was. Indians were here, and once more she had to hide in the cellar. She could hear two, perhaps three men above her. They seemed to be arguing.

Isaac listened so intently he did not even seem to be breathing. *What will he do?* Rebecca worried. *Will he turn me over to them?* She felt a sudden pang as she thought of her sister. *What will happen to Selinda if I never come back?*

Huddled in the dark, damp cellar, Rebecca crouched down in an agony of worry. Several more sets of footsteps passed close by. Then there was silence. Still Isaac did not move. Rebecca forced herself to remain quiet, too. She counted to one hundred, slowly. Then she could stand it no more.

"They've left," she whispered. "Let me out!"

"Shhhhh!" he answered abruptly. "A guard will come behind."

Rebecca bit her lip. Was this another of Isaac's tricks? But he was between her and the door. She had no choice but to wait. She began reciting scripture in her head. She was in the midst of the Twenty-third Psalm when once again she heard someone passing by on the ground above.

Yea, though I walk through the valley of the shadow of death, I will fear no evil, Rebecca prayed.

After the last footsteps faded away, Isaac waited still longer. Finally, he reached up and opened the cellar door a few inches. He looked out cautiously. Then he opened the door all the way and climbed out. Rebecca hurried after him.

"Who are they?" she asked in a low tone. "What are they doing?"

Isaac explained that the group was a raiding party from the north. They were not the same men who had attacked the Johnsons' farm but were another scouting party from that tribe.

"Why were they arguing?"

"Some wanted to raid a farm close to here," he said. "The leader said no, there was much danger from the enemy in the fort."

Rebecca was confused. "Enemy? What enemy?"

Isaac gave her an odd look. "Your soldiers, of course. The leader said they should return home. They go north now."

"But our soldiers aren't the enemy," Rebecca protested. "They protect us."

Isaac shook his head as if she were a particularly stupid child. He pulled his bundle out of the cellar, then shut the door.

Rebecca hesitated. She did not want to ask this question, but she had to know. "Were you part of that raid on the Johnsons' farm? Did you help capture that poor family?"

"No, I knew nothing of it," Isaac said.

Rebecca felt relieved, but his next words gave her a chill. "If I'd known, I would have escaped the fort. I would have traveled with them."

"Those savages kill people and take innocent families

captive! How could you want to join them?" Rebecca
exclaimed in horror.

"What about your soldiers?" Isaac shot back. "In the
village that they burned, they killed grandmothers, babies—
all were dead."

"If you like the Indians so much, why didn't you join
that raiding party that just passed?" Rebecca replied angrily.
"Why did you hide?"

Isaac looked at her stonily. "If I had come out, what
would have become of you?" he asked.

For a moment, Rebecca was stunned. Isaac had chosen
to protect her—even though it meant giving up his chance
to travel with the other Indians! She stared at him as he
picked up his small bundle, but his face was as blank as
ever. "I go to my family now," he said.

"Good-bye," Rebecca started to say, but Isaac had
already disappeared. Once again, she was left alone in
the wilderness.

In a daze, Rebecca turned and headed back to the fort.
With Indians so close by, she was afraid to walk through
the gloomy forest again. Instead, she decided to go down
to the river and follow it south, then climb back to the
fort on the same route she and Selinda had taken when
they had washed the quilts.

As she picked her way along the path, Rebecca thought about what she would do when she reached the fort. She knew it was her duty to go straight to the sentry. She should tell him that Isaac had escaped— and which route he had taken. But in her heart, she knew she could not do it. *He saved me,* she thought. *I cannot betray him.*

The rain was falling harder now, and the dusk was fading into the black of night. The sky was so cloudy that no stars were visible. There was only an occasional hint of moonlight. Rebecca stubbed her toe on a rock that she couldn't see on the path.

Once, she heard a rustle in the grass to her right. She dodged behind a tree and froze there. Then she saw a hawk fly up from the bushes with a small, struggling creature, probably a mouse, caught in its talons. *If I don't find the silver spoons, the Cutters are going to take Selinda away just like that hawk took the mouse,* she thought. *And there won't be anything I can do about it.*

She tried to think clearly: If Isaac hadn't stolen the spoons, who had? Could it have been Ezekiel? She knew now that Ezekiel had planted the knife in Isaac's bed just to cause trouble for the white Indian boy. Had Ezekiel hidden the knife—then gone up to the loft and looked for things to steal?

It was possible, perhaps, but Rebecca did not think it was likely. Ezekiel did not seem smart enough to both steal the spoons and plan a trap for Isaac. *But if Ezekiel's not the thief,* she wondered, *who could it be?*

Her mind was a jumble of questions as she found her way to the river, then continued her journey along its bank. There were fewer trees to act as shelters here, and the rain streamed onto her hair and face. She untied her Sunday apron and draped it over her head to act as a scarf. The river was easy to follow, and she walked quickly till she reached the trail that led to the South Gate.

She followed this trail through the woods until it emerged into the open meadow. She was almost across the meadow when she heard the soft whinny of a horse. A man on horseback came riding slowly out of the fog. Rebecca stood stock-still. The meadow was wide open. There was no place to run to.

The rider had not yet seen her. He was murmuring to his horse, "Come on, Betheulah, slow and quiet now. We'll be out of here before anyone knows we're gone."

Rebecca recognized that voice and hurried toward it. "Johnny!" she called out, and grabbed the horse's bridle. "Where are you going?"

The horse was frightened by her outburst and reared up slightly, but Rebecca held tight to its bridle. Old Johnny clutched his heart. "My word, girl, you nearly scared me to death," he exclaimed. "With that white thing over your head, I thought you was a ghost."

Rebecca pulled the apron off her head. "Where are

you going?" she asked the peddler. "You said you'd meet me at first light."

"I changed my mind," Johnny said. "I don't never stay no place long." He made a move as if to leave, but Rebecca continued to hold tight. Questions were forming in her mind.

"Johnny," she said. "You never came back to buy my silver spoons. Why?"

"Another time, child, another time," Johnny said. Again he made a move to leave, but Rebecca held on even tighter.

"You stole my spoons, didn't you, Johnny?" she accused him. "You tried to make me think that Isaac took them. But it was you. That's why you didn't come back to buy the spoons. You already had 'em. And that's why you didn't stay to meet me in the morning."

"You're talking nonsense, child. Let go of the bridle." He raised his hand as if to strike her.

Rebecca grasped the bridle even tighter. "No, I won't let go. Give me back my spoons or I'll scream so loud that the soldiers on patrol will hear me! I swear I will!"

Johnny hesitated. His hand fell. "I don't have 'em no more," he said at last. "I traded 'em for rum."

"My spoons!" Rebecca was outraged. "You traded them, then you drank the money?"

"A man gets a powerful thirst traveling out here, and you had no right to put temptation in my way," Johnny said, his voice becoming almost a whine. "You as much as told me you had them spoons in the loft, then you went outside to see about that white Indian boy. I decided to look at the spoons myself. I was goin' to give you the money for 'em someday."

"I want the money now," Rebecca demanded. "I need twenty-four shillings. You said they'd be worth even more than that."

"Very well, very well," the peddler grumbled.

He opened his pack and reached deep inside. He pulled out a small linen pouch. Rebecca squinted at it. Even in the darkness, she recognized the pouch that the spoons had been kept in. She held her breath as Johnny reached deeper into the pack and filled up the pouch, counting slowly. "One shilling, two, three . . ."

After he reached twenty-four, he tossed the pouch toward Rebecca. She released the bridle and tried to catch the money. She missed the pouch, and it fell on the grass.

"There, be gone with ye," Johnny said. He dug his heels into his horse's side, and Betheulah took off, galloping down the path and away from the fort.

Rebecca picked up the pouch and hefted it. It had a heavy, solid feel to it, but something seemed strange. It was too dark for Rebecca to see the coins, but she touched them with her fingers. Then, for the second time that night, she felt sick to her stomach. She realized it wasn't coins that Johnny had counted into the pouch so carefully. It was worthless old buttons.

She opened her mouth to scream for help, then she stopped. By the time the soldiers arrived and asked their questions, Johnny would be long gone. And she would have to do a great deal of explaining herself, especially when it was discovered that Isaac had run away.

I was a fool to have trusted Old Johnny, even for a moment, she thought to herself bitterly. *Now he's gone, and the spoons are gone. Soon Selinda will be gone, too.*

Rebecca had thought she was too big for crying, but somehow, tears began to roll down her cheeks. They blurred her vision, and as she walked across the meadow, she stumbled into a bush. Her skirt caught in its thorns. She tugged on it, and as she did, berries squished in her hand. She realized this was where she and Selinda had stopped several days before. Rebecca remembered how she had gathered blackberries at this bush, but Selinda had not wanted any because berries made her sick.

Rebecca had a sudden idea. She quickly filled her pockets with berries. Then she hurried toward the fort.

When she was close to the palisade, she hid in the shadows until she reached the gap at the corner where she had escaped earlier. She waited until she was sure no guards were about. Then she squeezed back through the palisade and into the fort.

CHAPTER 12

LEFT BEHIND

The church service had just ended. Settlers were straggling out of the Great Chamber, but the Gray family had not yet returned home. Rebecca was able to slip back through their lean-to and into the widow's house without anyone noticing her. She found that Widow Tyler was dozing, but Selinda was already home and pacing the floor.

"Where have you been?" Selinda asked. "I was so worried when I came home from church and did not see you or Isaac anywhere." She peered out the open door behind Rebecca. "Is he with you?"

Rebecca shut the door. "No," she whispered.

"Where is he?"

"If I tell you where he is, you'll have to lie about it if someone asks," Rebecca warned. "Do you want that?"

Selinda shook her head.

"Then I won't tell you until later, when it doesn't

matter," Rebecca said. "Come, we must act as if nothing is different."

Sundown of the Sabbath had passed, so the girls were able to do their chores. Rebecca warmed a pot of beans for their supper. She began to cook a big pan of cornbread to go with the beans. Then she remembered that Isaac was no longer there to eat his huge portions. She was surprised by the sudden pang of regret she felt.

The widow awoke and Rebecca served her supper in her chair. "I see Isaac is not eating with us tonight," the widow remarked.

"No, ma'am," Rebecca said. She busied herself cleaning up.

The widow fixed Rebecca with a sharp eye, but all she said was, "I see." Then she picked up her Bible and began reading it closely.

Later, the guard came by with his lantern. "I'm here to check on the boy," he announced. When he discovered Isaac was missing, he called an alarm and the fort was searched. Lieutenant Willard came to the house and questioned all of them. The widow explained that she had been sleeping and had no idea where the boy was. Selinda could honestly say that she knew nothing of the boy's whereabouts either.

Rebecca said that she didn't know where Isaac was or when he could have left. *That's only half a lie,* she told herself. *I really don't know where he is now.*

The guards reported that there was no sign of Isaac anywhere in the fort. Ezekiel, who had heard rumors of Isaac's disappearance, hurried to the widow's house to confirm them.

"Let's get him!" Ezekiel suggested to the guards when he found the rumors were true. "We can track him in the forest!"

Lieutenant Willard rejected the idea. "I've been hearing reports of another raiding party just north of here. My soldiers have all they can do to protect our families here. I'll not send my men out on a wild goose chase into the forest."

"But—" Ezekiel protested.

The lieutenant held up his hand. "No," he said firmly. "If that boy Isaac wants to die out there in the wilderness, so be it. I'll not go after him."

"Cowards!" Ezekiel murmured in a voice too low for Lieutenant Willard to hear. "I'm glad we're leaving here tomorrow."

Ezekiel turned to go, and Rebecca noticed that he was wearing a different knife on his belt. It was smaller than his old knife, and the handle looked old. *It serves Ezekiel right,* she thought. *If he hadn't tried to trap Isaac, he wouldn't have lost his knife.*

After the hubbub died down, Rebecca locked up the house, and she and Selinda climbed together up to their loft. There Rebecca told her sister everything that had happened in the forest that night—including her meeting with Old Johnny.

"The spoons are gone," she said at last. "I'm sorry."

"'Tis more important that you're safe," Selinda comforted her. "You were so brave—you could have been killed."

Rebecca nodded. "Isaac could have betrayed me to the Indians, but he didn't." She paused. "Mayhap you were right about him all along."

For a moment, both girls were quiet. Then Selinda asked, "What should we do now, Becca? Mrs. Cutter plans to leave the fort first thing tomorrow. She says she won't stay here a minute longer."

"Well," Rebecca began, "I have a plan . . ."

At daybreak the next morning, Mrs. Cutter knocked loudly on Widow Tyler's door and demanded that Selinda come out. "We must make an early start," she declared. "We have a long way to go before nightfall."

Rebecca opened the door, fear etched across her face. It had been a horrible night for both her and Selinda. There had been dark hours when Rebecca had felt sure she was going to lose her sister forever.

"Please, ma'am, won't you take money for Selinda's contract?" Rebecca begged Mrs. Cutter. "We collected sixteen shillings." She pointed to a pile of money neatly stacked on the table. "Selinda's so sick, I don't know as she'd survive the trip to Connecticut."

"Sick?" Mrs. Cutter demanded as she barged into the house. "What do you mean, sick?"

Widow Tyler was sitting in her chair. She looked up as Mrs. Cutter stomped into the house. "Good morning, Amelia," she said. "Godspeed on your journey."

Mrs. Cutter ignored her. She turned on Rebecca, anger blazing from her blue eyes. "Is this more of your foolishness, Rebecca? I won't be trifled with. Let me see the girl."

"She's in bed and she's awful sick, ma'am," Rebecca said desperately. She stood in front of the ladder to the sleeping loft. "Maybe you shouldn't go up there."

Mrs. Cutter was determined. She pushed Rebecca out of the way and climbed the ladder to the loft. As Rebecca hurried up the ladder behind her, she heard Mrs. Cutter call out, "Selinda! You get up from that bed right now!"

But when she reached the bed, Mrs. Cutter gasped. Selinda's face was covered with red welts, her eyelids were puffed up, and her lips were so thick she could barely speak.

Mrs. Cutter covered her hand with her handkerchief, then carefully pulled back Selinda's quilt. Selinda's arms and legs were red and swollen with welts.

"Selinda," Mrs. Cutter asked, her voice less sure now, "is this some sort of trick? Are you truly ailing?"

"Oh, ma'am," Selinda mumbled through her swollen lips. "I feel awful."

Rebecca scratched her own arms. "I don't feel so good myself," she said. "I sure hope 'tisn't the pox."

Mrs. Cutter stepped away and hurriedly climbed back down the ladder. Rebecca followed after her.

"I suppose it wouldn't do to expose other people to a sick servant," Mrs. Cutter said as she scooped the money off the table. "I've come to a decision, Rebecca. Your sister may stay here with you."

Mrs. Cutter shut the door firmly behind her.

Rebecca climbed back up to see her sister. "Mrs. Cutter is gone now," she announced. "We needn't worry. How are you?"

Selinda groaned. "I did not lie," she mumbled. "I *do* feel awful."

"I know," said Rebecca. "I'm sorry. I never dreamed you'd get so sick. Last night, you swelled up so much I thought you'd die. I prayed all night for you to live. And you *are* better now, aren't you?"

Selinda nodded. Her puffed lips parted in a slight smile. "And now I'm free. It's a miracle. Thank you, Becca."

"We should thank Isaac," Rebecca said. "He gave me the idea. He told me about a boy who escaped from the Indians by pretending to be sick. I figured you might escape from Mrs. Cutter the same way." She patted her sister's arm. "I'll fetch you some water. 'Twill make you feel better."

Rebecca climbed back downstairs. She was pouring her sister a cup of water when she heard a chuckle. She turned.

Widow Tyler was sitting in her chair, laughing to herself. "Selinda never could eat berries, could she, Rebecca?"

"No, ma'am, she never could, and I'll never give them to her again, either. It 'most killed her," Rebecca said. Then she smiled. "But it worked, didn't it? Mrs. Cutter was so scared she almost broke out in a rash herself."

"Yes, indeed," the widow agreed, chuckling again. "It was a sight for sore eyes."

"May we stay on with you, ma'am?" Rebecca asked the widow. "Selinda can sew things for money, and I'll do whatever jobs I can."

"You may stay as long as you want, dear," Widow Tyler said, still smiling. "As long as you want."

By the time Captain Stevens and his men returned to the fort, the days had grown chilly and the trees on the hills had turned a bright patchwork of orange, gold, and flaming red. The captain told the fort's settlers that he had traveled to Portsmouth, where he'd asked New Hampshire's colonial governor for more troops to protect the frontier settlements.

When he learned that Isaac had run away, Captain Stevens was saddened but not surprised. "I'd hoped the boy could rejoin his white family," he said, "but I feared it might be too late."

Soon after the captain arrived, he paid a call at Widow Tyler's house. Rebecca told him all—or almost all—about the thefts in the fort, including how Old Johnny had stolen the silver spoons.

Captain Stevens listened gravely, then said, "If Johnny ever comes back this way, we'll make him pay for your spoons, I promise." He paused, then added, "As for Isaac, I don't s'pose we'll ever see him again."

"Why did he go back to the Indians, sir?" Rebecca asked. Ever since Isaac had left, that question had worried her. "Why did he choose them over us?"

For a long moment, the captain was silent. He looked out the cabin's back window toward the red and gold trees that colored the hills beyond Fort Number 4. "The way we live here at the fort is not the only way to live, Rebecca," he said at last. "The Indians have their own ways, and if you knew them as I do, and as Isaac does, you'd respect them. As I told you before, the Indians are not savages, they're people—and Isaac has come to love them like family. Can you understand that?"

Rebecca's cheeks burned. *I wasn't kind to Isaac,* she thought. *But he saved my life anyway. A savage would not have done that.*

"Aye, sir," she said quietly. She looked out at the vividly colored trees. With the arrival of autumn, she knew that the first frost—and the first snow—could not be far away. "Do you think Isaac will make it back to the Indians?" she asked.

The captain frowned thoughtfully. "He has a good chance. He knows the woods. And a man can travel a long way if he knows he's going home."

Home! Rebecca thought. Isaac had talked about this land as being the Indians' home. But didn't it really belong to the settlers? She was no longer sure.

"I hope he returns home safe," said Selinda. She walked toward them using the cane Isaac had made for her. "He missed his family."

The captain smiled. "Speaking of returning home, while I was in Portsmouth, Governor Wentworth gave me an express from Governor Shirley of the Massachusetts Bay Colony. He received this from Canada." He pulled a carefully folded piece of parchment out of his pocket. As he opened it, Rebecca's heart beat faster. The crackly yellow paper was filled with elegant but faded writing. Rebecca peered at it closely, but she couldn't make out the words.

"What does it say?" she asked impatiently. "I can't read it."

"It's French," said the captain. He pointed halfway down the page. "Maybe ye can read this."

Rebecca squinted at the loops and curls. She was able to understand two words: *Josiah Percy.* She looked up at the captain. "What does it mean?"

"The governor of Massachusetts received a list of captives that the Indians have traded to the French," he explained. "The people on this list are now in prison in Canada, and the governor is bargaining for their release. The French terms are high, but I think we'll come to an understanding." He held his finger under *Percy.* "That says 'Josiah Percy with wife and young son.'"

"They're . . . they're alive!" Rebecca exclaimed. She felt weak with relief. "They're coming home!"

"It may take some time," Captain Stevens cautioned. "But the governor is doing his best. With luck, we may be able to bring them home before the river freezes over."

Selinda's face flushed with excitement. "Oh, Rebecca, you were right!" she exclaimed as she hugged her sister. "You always said they'd come back to us!"

Rebecca felt a surge of joy. *They're really coming home!* she thought. She stood a little straighter and smiled at her sister. "Of course, they're coming back! Mama promised they would!"

A Peek into the Past

LOOKING BACK: 1754

Indian attacks were one of the colonists' greatest fears.

In 1754, the northern frontier of New England was a difficult, dangerous place for colonial girls like Rebecca Percy. Far from the comforts and protection of towns, English settlers struggled to clear forests, plant crops, and build homes. Settlers faced many dangers, but they feared most being killed or captured by Indians.

The danger was very real. In the century before the American Revolution, more than 1,600 New England colonists were taken captive, just as Rebecca's parents and brother were. Many captives never saw their homes and families again.

Like Rebecca, most English colonists viewed Indians as "savages" invading their land. Refusing to give up their newly settled territory, the English built small forts like Fort Number 4 along the frontier. In these isolated outposts, all the families in the area knew and depended on one another. The fort was the center of their lives—the place where they worshiped, visited, and traded together. It was also their gathering place in times of danger.

What the settlers did not want to accept was that

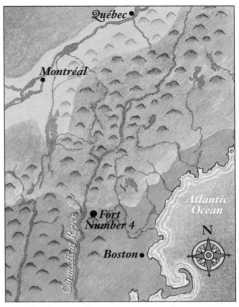

Areas of English settlement in 1754 are shown in orange, French in yellow. Indians, including the Abenakis, were being squeezed into the green areas.

Native Americans had first claims on the land. The frontier "wilderness" was home to thousands of Indians living in strong, established societies, such as the Mohawks and the Senecas in New York and the Abenakis in Vermont, New Hampshire, and Maine. They lived in villages of bark-covered houses, planted crops of corn, beans, and squash, fished and canoed along the rivers, and hunted and trapped in the forests for food and clothing as well as furs to trade with the French in Canada.

As English settlers pushed north and west, clearing forests and fencing land, they destroyed the hunting grounds that Native Americans depended on. Some Indians chose to move farther north or west—into territory claimed by other Indian people—but many decided to stay and fight for the land that had been theirs.

The French in nearby Canada spurred the Indians on. The French wanted to keep their long-time enemies, the English, from

A typical Indian village before settlers came to New England

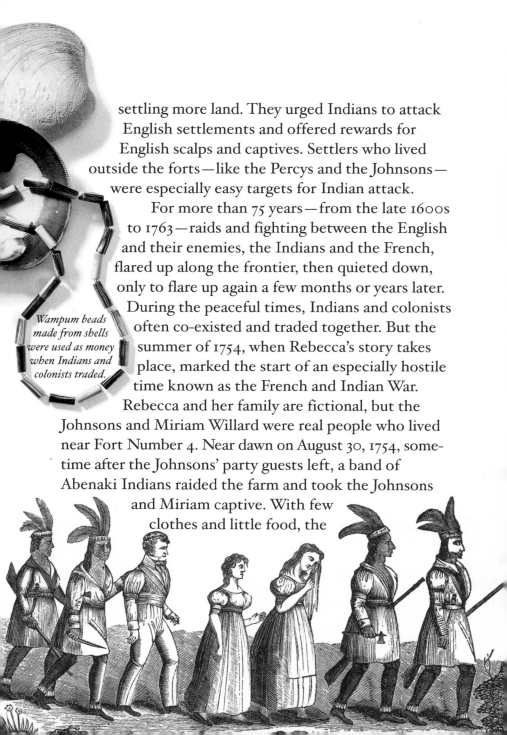

settling more land. They urged Indians to attack English settlements and offered rewards for English scalps and captives. Settlers who lived outside the forts—like the Percys and the Johnsons—were especially easy targets for Indian attack.

For more than 75 years—from the late 1600s to 1763—raids and fighting between the English and their enemies, the Indians and the French, flared up along the frontier, then quieted down, only to flare up again a few months or years later. During the peaceful times, Indians and colonists often co-existed and traded together. But the summer of 1754, when Rebecca's story takes place, marked the start of an especially hostile time known as the French and Indian War.

Rebecca and her family are fictional, but the Johnsons and Miriam Willard were real people who lived near Fort Number 4. Near dawn on August 30, 1754, some-time after the Johnsons' party guests left, a band of Abenaki Indians raided the farm and took the Johnsons and Miriam captive. With few clothes and little food, the

Wampum beads made from shells were used as money when Indians and colonists traded.

Indians and their captives began the long march over rough forest trails to Canada.

On the second day of the march, Susanna Johnson gave birth to her fourth child, a daughter she named "Captive." The Abenakis often killed captives who couldn't keep up with the group, and Susanna feared she and her baby would die. But, although the Abenakis were often harsh with the Johnsons, they also

Susanna Johnson showed kindness. Even when they themselves were hungry, the Abenakis shared their food, and they helped carry the Johnson children through parts of the trip. Somehow, everyone in the group survived the three-week journey.

Abenakis usually sold their captives to the French, who then traded or sold the prisoners back to the English. That was what happened to Miriam Willard and most of the Johnsons.

Six-year-old Sylvanus Johnson, however, was adopted by the Abenakis. Some captives, especially children, were taken into Indian families to replace members killed by war or epidemics of European diseases such as smallpox and measles.

Indians often treated adopted captives as true sons or daughters, dressing them in Indian clothes and teaching them their language and customs. Like the

Many captives were treated harshly, but others—like this child—were shown kindness and generosity.

Cornplanter, the son of a Seneca mother and a white captive, became a respected warrior and chief.

fictional Isaac, many captives came to think of themselves as Indians and became full members of Indian society. These "white Indians" often refused to return to their blood relatives, even when given the chance. Some, like Isaac, were brought back to the white world but ran away again to rejoin their Indian families.

Some "white Indians" did return permanently to colonial society. Sylvanus Johnson was brought back to New England when he was 11. At first, he did not even recognize his mother. Gradually, he relearned English ways, but he kept a lifelong respect for the Abenakis.

Captives who returned to the colonies sometimes acted as ambassadors between the two cultures. Captain Phineas Stevens, for example, was a real person captured by Abenakis as a teenager. Although he was ransomed by his father and returned to the colonies, he never forgot his Indian "father," and he traded with Native Americans throughout his life. Because of his knowledge of Indians, Stevens was sent on government missions to Canada to *redeem,* or ransom, other captives.

The Indians were not the only ones who took captives. The English also captured Indians during raids and battles. Usually captured Indians were traded for English

This statue honors Mary Jemison. Captured as a girl in 1757, she chose to live out her life as a Seneca wife and mother.

prisoners or were kept as slaves or servants in colonists' homes. (As Rebecca and Selinda knew well, many English families kept *indentured servants*, workers who were required by law to serve their master for a given term—often five to seven years, or even more.) Writers of the time, including Benjamin Franklin, noted that Native American captives—unlike white captives—*always* wanted to return to their own people.

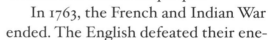

An indentured servant working for a glassmaker

In 1763, the French and Indian War ended. The English defeated their enemies and won control of Canada. Indians retreated from the English settlers, and peace came to New England. But the war had taught American colonists that they could work together against a common enemy. Twelve years later, when the colonists decided they no longer wanted to be ruled by a king in faraway London, they banded together to fight a new war: the American Revolution.

AUTHOR'S NOTE

Isaac's account of a captive who escaped the Indians by pretending to be sick is based on an actual event. It's important to note, though, that Rebecca's similar plan for her sister was very risky. Allergic reactions such as Selinda's can be serious and can even cause death.

In researching this book, I read many fascinating true stories from the French and Indian wars. I owe a debt of gratitude to all the historians who helped me understand this dangerous but exciting period in American history. My special thanks to Colin G. Calloway, Professor of History and Native American Studies at Dartmouth College and author of many books, including *North Country Captives* and, for younger readers, *The Abenaki*. Professor Calloway's research provided valuable insights into Native American culture and the experiences of captives. Readers interested in historical fiction may enjoy Elizabeth George Speare's *Calico Captive,* which tells the imagined adventures of Miriam Willard after her capture.

I'm grateful to the staff and volunteers of the Fort at No. 4 Living History Museum in Charlestown, New Hampshire, especially Barbara Bullock Jones, the fort's historian, Roberto M. Rodriguez, the fort's director, and his assistant, Elizabeth Petke. The reconstructed fort in Charlestown vividly shows life in a New England frontier settlement in the mid-1700s, and it helped me imagine what it would have been like to have been Rebecca Percy—or Isaac Davidson.

ABOUT THE AUTHOR

Sarah Masters Buckey grew up in New Jersey, where her
favorite hobbies were swimming in the summer, sled-
ding in the winter, and reading all year round. Whenever
her family packed their car for vacations, her mother would
include a grocery bag filled with books just for her.

As a writer, she's enjoyed living and working in different
parts of the United States, including fifteen years in Texas.
She and her husband and their three children now make
their home in New Hampshire, in a house a few blocks from
the Connecticut River. She is also the author of another
History Mystery, *The Smuggler's Treasure*.

FREE CATALOGUE!

Welcome to a world that's all yours—because it's filled with the things girls love! Beautiful dolls that capture your heart. Books that send your imagination soaring. And games and pastimes that make being a girl great!

For your **free** AmericanGirl® catalogue, return this postcard, call **1-800-845-0005,** or visit our Web site at **americangirl.com**.

Send me a catalogue:

My name

My address

City   State   Zip 12583i

My birth date: _____ / _____ / _____
           month day year

Send my friend a catalogue:

My friend's name

Address

City   State   Zip 12591i

My e-mail address

Parent's signature

If you love Amelia, you'll love *American Girl* magazine!

For just $19.95, we'll send you 6 big bimonthly issues of *American Girl.* You'll get games, giggles, crafts, projects, and helpful advice. Plus, you'll find Amelia in every issue!

Yes!
I want to order a subscription.
❑ Bill me ❑ Payment enclosed

Send bill to: (please print)

Adult's name

Address

City   State   Zip

Send magazine to: (please print)

Girl's name

Address

City   State   Zip

Guarantee: You may cancel anytime for a full refund. Allow 4–6 weeks for first issue. Canadian subscription $24 U.S. © 2001 Pleasant Company K11L1